PERSUADED
BY THE
Billionaire

ROSE M. COOPER

OSHUN
PUBLICATIONS
oshunpublications.com

Published by Oshun Publications
701 Market Street Suite 110-6035
Saint Augustine, FL 32095
www.oshunpublications.com

Disclaimer
This is a work of fiction. Names, characters, places, and incidents either are the product of the author's imagination or are used fictitiously. Any resemblance to actual persons, living or dead, events, or locales is entirely coincidental.

Book design by oliviaprodesign
www.fiverr.com/oliviaprodesign

ISBN 978-1-956319-58-3 (Paperback)
ISBN 978-1-956319-59-0 (Hardback)
ISBN 978-1-956319-57-6 (eBook)

JOIN MY NEWSLETTER
GET UPDATES,
FREEBIES & SPECIALS
rosemaecooper.com/newsletter

Titles Available As Audiobook

rosemaecooper.com/audiobooks

Searching for Bliss

GISSELLE PHILLIPS SAT on her yoga mat, her body maintaining a perfect lotus pose. She held an auralite crystal in her left hand. It was supposed to help her find a more profound feeling of serenity and open her mind to receiving more positive energy. She held a small citrine stone in her right hand to attract success and infuse her with positive energy. The positivity was there, but deep serenity seemed to elude her today. At least the success part appeared to connect with her. She had spent a busy week at her very important job, and now that she had made it to Friday evening, she really needed to relieve her stress. Not that she didn't love her job. Being the director of a nonprofit organization was very rewarding—but at the same time, it was all-encompassing and took a lot out of her.

She smiled softly and inhaled deeply, imagining that her thick, curly, glossy black hair was pulled gently up and back into a high, tight ponytail, sucking out all her thoughts and tying her worries neatly into her silk scrunchie. The warm California sun was penetrating the windows of her backyard solarium, warming her skin, caressing her, making her feel safe and happy. She could feel the soft padding of the mat beneath her and imagined herself sitting close to the ocean. Near enough to feel touches of salt spray upon her skin, her body supported by the warm sands of Malibu just steps away from her childhood home. She willed her mind to be quiet to achieve her desired state of mindfulness.

She visualized herself on the beach. Thinking of nothing other than the soothing sound of the waves touching the shore and feeling the warmth of the sun on her back, a soft breeze kissing her long legs as it swept over her. Most of the time, Gisselle could find her bliss, empty her mind of thoughts and worries, and repeat her daily mantras in her head. Unfortunately, try as she might, today was not one of those days. Images of work deadlines swarmed her thoughts, and she couldn't let go of her stress long enough to fall into a productive meditation session.

At just twenty-six years old, Gisselle had already achieved a level of career success that most women only dreamed of. She earned her Master of Social Welfare Degree at UCLA the previous year. Her current career path was completely different from how she had been raised. Gisselle's personality was humble and unassuming. One would never guess that she had grown up in Los Angeles, surrounded by film and television industry people, and descended from Hollywood royalty. To an outsider, Gisselle's life might have appeared surreal. It was so storybook perfect. Yet, despite having access to the best runway coaches, acting classes, and agents, that wasn't Gisselle's calling. Even her social media presence was minimal. She couldn't explain it other than to say that she didn't crave that kind of attention. Maybe the knowledge that access to that celebrity world was proximate and available to her anytime she wanted. Making her want to keep it all at arm's length instead of chasing it.

Not that she wasn't proud of it–her grandmother had

been the first African American actress to win a daytime Emmy award and an Oscar in the same year. When she took Gisselle to school, all the mothers immediately recognized her, and they lost their minds. The attention almost made Gisselle uncomfortable. Her grandmother had explained that when people watched you on television every week, and your image and voice were actually a regular presence in their home, some people felt a closeness to you that, although imagined, seemed real to them, and this is why they had no problem coming right up and talking to you. She also reminded Gisselle that it was always important to appreciate your fans because, without them, nobody would watch your movies or your shows on television or "these new streaming services."

Gisselle had grown up very close to her grandmother, and they had remained tight until the very end. They really understood one another, and you might say that Gisselle was an old soul. She was so wise and introspective. In her last year of college, Gisselle had moved in with her grandmother, assisted with her care, and had actually been holding her hand in hospice when she recently passed away. Despite her absence, her grandmother's spirit was always with her. In fact, the place where she was sitting at that very moment was the same Spanish-tiled solarium where she and her grandmother used to enjoy tea together on an almost daily basis. When her grandmother died, she had left Gisselle her Art Deco-style house in Hancock Park, a very upscale suburb of Los Angeles, along with more than enough money to keep her comfortable for the rest of her life.

Both of Gisselle's parents had spent their lives in the limelight too, and their careers were still going strong. As a child, she used to follow them to sets sometimes. She had always enjoyed watching the process of her mother transforming into another character in the hair and makeup chair and then trying on some fancy wardrobe to compliment her new look.

In her teenage years, she used to accompany her parents to awards shows and other red carpet events, and she genuinely loved the glitz and glamor of it all. Her parents had perhaps imagined that she would follow in their Hollywood footsteps. However, despite being 5'9" tall, long and slender, with classically pretty features, she wasn't interested in following in her model-turned-actress mother's footsteps. Gisselle had always felt that there was a different kind of purpose for her.

As for her father, he was a career actor who had dabbled in movies, but his bread and butter was his decades-long role as the police commissioner on a daytime soap opera. That role had given their family financial stability over the years, and Gisselle loved running lines with him—but acting just wasn't her thing. Maybe the fact that she had been exposed to Hollywood life for as far back as she could remember, to the point where it was her normal, had rendered it less exciting to her. Whatever the reason, Gisselle had opted to follow an academic path with a view to give back. She recognized her privilege, and she wanted to uplift those who had fewer opportunities for advancement.

Throughout her college years, Gisselle had volunteered with several charity organizations, but the one she had really identified with was The Elevated World, an organization that connected underprivileged children with the opportunity to put their hands on books and to experience the joy of reading for fun. When she began working on her master's degree, she started an internship there, and the whole experience opened her eyes to a world that she had never before conceived of. There were so many children in the Los Angeles area from all different backgrounds whose parents either couldn't take them to the library, didn't have the means to buy them books, or were illiterate themselves. Even today, years later, Gisselle remembered with a smile the first day she had driven the bookmobile through the ghettos of L.A. From the moment that

Gisselle's eyes had looked into the openly joyous face of an eight year old girl as she selected her first book that was just for her, she was hooked. There was no going anywhere else for Gisselle; she had found her calling.

As she tried once more to control her breathing and to clear her mind of thoughts and worries, she heard the unmistakable sound of her longtime friend Indi Priest's no-nonsense voice.

"Gisselle, are you in the backyard?" Startled, Gisselle opened her eyes to see that Indi was knocking on the glass door of the solarium. She heaved a sigh of resignation–she wasn't going to find her yogic bliss today. Slowly, she stood up, stretching her long, toned legs into a standing position. Not expecting company, all she wore was a pair of leggings and a matching sports bra. Undeterred, Indi kept knocking.

"Hi Indi, come on inside, let me make us some herbal tea," Gisselle spoke softly to her friend, hoping she would dial down her energy. Also twenty-six years old, Indi lived next door with her parents, both high-powered Hollywood producers. The women had known each other all their lives, and over the past few years, the women had grown to be good friends, despite the fact that they were total opposites.

Indi was petite and high-energy. She be-bopped around with her fair skin, brown eyes, and long chestnut brown hair. She had the most perfect little figure, and she knew how to make the most of it. Today, Indi wore a floral romper and high-heeled espadrilles, her hair tied up into an optimistic ponytail. Indi was more of a free spirit than Gisselle and had worked very hard to earn herself a reputation as one of L.A.'s top hair and makeup artists. She was also known for only dating famous men, namely the actors whose makeup she did for movies and television series.

"Elle, I'm going to need something stronger than tea," Indi replied, a serious scowl on her face. "Nathan just dumped me. Can you believe it? Once again, I fell for a man who took advantage of my industry connections to advance his career, and then poof! We're done!"

"Oh, honey," Gisselle lamented, empathizing with her friend. "What happened this time?"

"He landed a role on a series that's shooting in New York City, and he didn't want to be tied down. Nice! He didn't mind being tied down last weekend with my silk Hermès scarf."

"Oh dear," began Gisselle.

"I really thought that Nathan was going to go the distance. Then, to add insult to injury, last night on TMZ, they showed a story about him and his guest star of the week fornicating in a tatami room at that new sushi bar in Sherman Oaks. Sherman Oaks—can you believe it? I mean, if you're going to do that, at least have the class to do it at Nobu in West Hollywood," Indi was really wound up. "Sherman Oaks! There's no dignity."

"Wow," replied Gisselle. "I didn't watch the entertainment news last night. So sorry, hon. I didn't see that one coming, either. I can totally see why you're upset. He's a big jerk."

"And a fame whore," Indi concurred. "He knew or ought to have known that TMZ would be following him. I think he wanted to be caught in flagrante delicto. I'm such a fool. Almost two years together, and I still didn't predict this. I need to figure out how to become a better judge of character. It's clear I'm lacking in that regard."

"Indi, let's be real. You haven't taken a break from dating for as long as I've known you," stated Gisselle. "Have you ever thought of stopping to inhale, just taking a short break from men, so that you can get to know yourself better from the inside? Maybe you would benefit from some time to yourself, and then you'll have a better chance at choosing the right partner next time."

"LOL," replied Indi, rolling her eyes. "Yeah, I don't think so. It's been my experience that the very best kind of self-exploration is the kind that happens when there is a very big, very hard, and very persistent dick inside of you."

Although her last name was Priest, it was clear that Indi had nothing holy or chaste about her. She loved men, she wholeheartedly enjoyed sex, and she wasn't afraid who knew. "So I need my best friend to get out of her yoga pants, put on a very short slip dress, some four inch high-heeled sandals, lip gloss, and a smile so that we can go out tonight and have fun!" The look on Indi's face told Gisselle that she meant business, and she wasn't going to leave without an assurance from her friend that they were going to get dolled up to go out tonight.

There was no question that Gisselle was utterly exhausted from a long week at work, and that thoughts about her administrative duties were swirling around inside her mind. However, she could tell that her friend really needed companionship tonight, and she couldn't let her down. Would she rather stay home tonight and curl up with a glass of wine and a trashy romance novel? Absolutely, but Gisselle wasn't the type to let a friend down. Plus, her new cage sandals were sitting on a shelf in her closet, practically begging to be worn.

"Fine," Gisselle conceded. "Just give me time to have a quick shower, put on some makeup, and get dressed."

"Okay, I'll check back in an hour?" Indi asked.

"Yes, I'll be ready," promised Gisselle, laughing. "Now, let's both go get gorgeous!"

Man on the Run

Kʏʟᴀɴ Mᴜʀʀᴀʏ ᴡᴀs ᴇɴᴊᴏʏɪɴɢ this stage of his life. The hard part was over, and now he could just sail through and enjoy himself. While it's true that he may have been uncommonly lucky, what's also true is that the harder he worked, the luckier he seemed to get. He stood up from his desk, poured himself a glass of scotch neat, and strode over to look out the wall of floor-to-ceiling glass windows. The early evening sun shone through the glass. It warmed him, counteracting the cooling sensation of the perpetually air-conditioned space. He loved the view from his 26th-floor office space, which seemed to pan across all Los Angeles.

Growing up in the suburb of Van Nuys, his parents, who were both teachers, had taught him the value of a dollar and the importance of getting a solid education. Kylan had followed through in that regard, earning his MBA from the Stanford Graduate School of Business. He had spent the better part of his twenties working his way up in the technology and innovation sector and enjoying the excitement surrounding technology startups reverberating throughout Silicon Valley. Perhaps most importantly, Kylan loved the San

Francisco party scene. The restaurants were second to none, and the nightclubs were very happening and filled with women falling all over themselves to try and tie him down.

As one of only a few African American men in his graduating class at Stanford, he had always been aware that he stood out. He was 6'2" tall, with lean muscles and a soft face. Kylan's parents had taught him to always be quietly respectful. To listen more than he spoke at meetings, build bridges, and cultivate relationships with the right people. This meant that, in addition to his intellectual ability, he had developed a keen sense of self and the ability to read people. He could tell when someone was being sincere and when they were blowing smoke. This spidey sense of his had served him well in business, as well as in his interpersonal relationships. Kylan did not suffer fools gladly.

Two years ago, just before his thirtieth birthday, a professional opportunity presented, prompting him to move home to Los Angeles. One of his professors had paired up with a small group of investors. They invited Kylan to become a founder of a new venture capitalist group based in LA. Along with this unique opportunity came a certain level of risk. It had taken Kylan a long while to finally decide to take the plunge and start his own company with his fellow founding partners. Luckily for Kylan, he had always been cautious with his money. He invested conservatively, which allowed him to leave his comfort zone of Silicon Valley and start fresh. The old Kylan was focused on the proverbial rat race and had been on a mission to earn his first million dollars. Now, he had parlayed his talent and experience into a level of wealth that he had never before thought possible. Instead of focusing on how much money he could earn this year, he was now in the very fortunate position of being able to ask himself how much he could give away.

He heard his office line ring and snapped out of his

daydream. He stepped over to his desk, put down his drink, and pressed the button to answer the call on speaker. "Kylan Murray here," he said.

"Kylan, it's Mateo," he recognized his financial planner's voice on the other end of the call. "Have you had a chance to review your quarterly investment statements? Your portfolio has gone up by 19% over the past three months. You're practically swimming in dividends. Do you want to give away some of this money, or shall I just reinvest it?"

"I appreciate the follow-up, my man," Kylan's tone was casual now. "I've been looking into charitable organizations, and I think I'd like to stay local this year. There's a non-profit called The Elevated World, where it's all about delivering books to underprivileged kids in the LA area. Have you heard of that one?"

"Yes, actually, I have," replied Mateo. "My wife and I just went to a fundraiser for them. They do more than just the bookmobile. The Elevated World offers a full literacy program for school-aged children, with free tutoring and everything. That's a good one. Your money will definitely be put to good use there. You won't regret it."

"Thank you. Yeah, that sounds good to me. Like a worthwhile cause. Do you think two million is the right amount this time? A nice, round number?" asked Kylan.

"Yes, I'll do the math to make sure," said Mateo. "I think that should offset your gains, and you're making a difference to kids here in LA. It's a win-win. I'll double-check the numbers, and if everything looks correct, I'll make that contribution on your behalf. Fair?"

"That sounds just right. Thanks again, Mateo." Kylan felt secure knowing that his financial planner was always paying attention and offering him the right kind of advice.

"You bet," replied Mateo, and they ended their call.

Glancing at his solid gold Patek Philippe watch, Kylan

realized it was already past 6:00 p.m. He texted his friend, Pierce James, to see if he was interested in meeting for dinner. His friend answered immediately, advising him that he had already secured a reservation at Catch Steak. That's perfect, thought Kylan, and he messaged his driver to pick him up downstairs. He swallowed the last drink, put on his blazer, and went downstairs to the lobby.

As soon as he stepped outside, he spotted his driver parked in the passenger zone, waiting for him to arrive.

"Thank you, Atticus," said Kylan as he stepped into the white Cadillac Escalade. "I'm meeting Pierce at Catch Steak."

"Very good, Mr. Murray," Atticus replied, closing the door quietly, then getting into the driver's seat. "I trust you had a good day at work."

"Yes, Atticus, I feel like I've done some good today. Thank you for asking," Kylan answered thoughtfully.

The rest of the drive was quiet, and Kylan scrolled through his Twitter and Instagram feeds just to pass the time. On Twitter, he looked up The Elevated World. He noticed they had just posted a feature about a young woman named Gisselle Phillips, who had recently become the organization's new director. The image of Gisselle captivated him for a reason that he couldn't quite pinpoint. It was an unretouched photo, a picture of her smiling as she handed out books to young children. Did she look familiar? Was that it? He was trying to figure out if they had met somewhere, maybe in school or the LA party scene.

"We have arrived, Mr. Murray," Atticus's voice interrupted his thoughts, and he unfastened his seat belt, then stepped his long legs out of the vehicle.

"Thank you, Atticus. I'll send you a text when I'm ready to go home," Kylan told him.

"Very good, sir," Atticus nodded, then got back into the vehicle and drove away.

When Kylan arrived at the hostess' table, he opened his mouth to speak. Still, he didn't have to because the woman immediately recognized him and directed him to his table, where Pierce was already seated, waiting for him.

"My man," Pierce said as he got up, and they shared a fist pump and a man hug. Kylan laughed, then sat down opposite his friend.

The men had known each other since their childhood days in Van Nuys. They had been next-door neighbors, and their parents had always been friends, so they had practically grown up together. Their parents still lived in those same homes, next to one another. Even though the boys fit in well and got along with all the neighborhood kids, it had been a comfort to have another African American family right next door. Pierce had always been his wingman; after all this time, the two men had perfected their catch and release technique.

While Pierce hadn't achieved quite the same level of financial success as Kylan, he was still doing alright. He had transformed himself from a skinny, nerdy teenage boy into Dr. Pierce James, ophthalmologist to the stars. In reality, he treated patients from all walks of life. However, when he was talking up the ladies, he tended to embellish his stories about emergency eye surgeries from something going wrong on a movie set without giving out any identifying details. That was just part of his shtick.

Pierce loved every minute of being a wealthy, single doctor in LA. He had bought himself a penthouse in West Hollywood, and it seemed like he had a new weekly girlfriend. Although, Pierce would never use the term "girlfriend." He was delighted to be a bachelor and had no plans to settle down. Kylan agreed; however, that online image of Gisselle Phillips triggered some interesting feeling in him. It's not like he suddenly needed to get married, but when he looked at her smiling face, he realized there might be more to life than dating.

"Is the night ending here, or will you come with me to Skybar tonight at the Mondrian?" Pierce asked with a grin.

"Oh, we can do the Skybar, but first, I'm ordering a juicy T-bone steak, medium-well," Kylan said with a smile.

"Ditto for me, and then we'll go find some honeys at the Skybar," Pierce licked his lips.

"Okay, my brother, but let's just hope there are some new faces there tonight because I'm done sampling one another's leftovers," Kylan shook his head. "In fact, my days of sampling may be coming to an end."

"If you say so, but there's no way I'm letting myself get snared, not even if she's a Kardashian, yo!" Pierce was laughing.

"I hear you, my friend. Don't get me wrong—I do enjoy the attention. Still, I'm thinking I might be ready for a woman of substance," Kylan wasn't suggesting that he needed to get married tomorrow. Still, he was definitely losing his patience with the bimbos who really just wanted to get in and enjoy his lifestyle. It had been fun for a long time, but it had started to wear thin lately.

"No problem, big guy. That leaves more for me," said Pierce, with a wink.

They finished their meal, paid their bill, and walked a few blocks to the Mondrian Hotel, where the Skybar awaited them. This was their favorite rooftop patio. It was known to be a hangout for models, actors, and lots of new money. This was a place to see and be seen, but tonight Kylan just wanted to have a good time with his friend. The night air was sultry, and Kylan felt a tingle of excitement at the prospect of meeting someone new. The cynic in him thought it would probably be the typical crowd of social climbers who would recognize him. This is where, for Kylan, social media was a bit of a curse. People and businesses tagged him in their posts and stories. While he couldn't deny that he liked the ego boost, he was concerned about maintaining his credibility in the venture capitalist world. Maybe tonight, he could just chill with Pierce and fly under the radar.

The two men found a high table near the periphery of the bar. Pierce liked a panoramic view of the space, and Kylan preferred to be on the fringe so they could maintain a conversation. As soon as their server took their order—two dirty martinis, extra dry—Kylan spotted his ex-girlfriend Shay Armstrong. Their eyes locked, and even though he acknowledged her and deliberately looked away, she shamelessly stalked her five-inch stiletto heels directly over to their table.

Pierce could see that his friend was cringing a little, but he didn't say anything just yet. He was transfixed by Shay's appearance. She was petite and curvy, with full, round bosoms, a tiny waist, and a high, tight ass that a man could really have fun with. Her smooth, dark, chocolaty skin glistened with a touch of perspiration in the evening light. Tonight, she wore a slinky bright yellow dress that showed off every curve, with a side slit that came almost up to her waist and revealed that she might not be wearing any panties. Shaking his head, Pierce struggled to understand why his best friend would decline such a delicious-looking opportunity.

"Kylan Murray," began Shay, in a chastising tone, "How come you don't call me anymore?"

"Hi Shay," his tone wasn't friendly at all. "I believe I haven't called you because we broke up three months ago. Remember?"

Kylan should have known from the start that Shay was a gold digger. By day, she was a dental hygienist and fancied herself as a social media influencer by night. He had been reluctant to date her initially, but Shay could be very persuasive. Luckily for Kylan, his assistant had shown him her Instagram stories once. She gave her followers a tutorial on how to land a rich man, using him as an example. That had completely turned him off of her and had left him with a bad taste in his mouth. He had ended things without an explanation, which was inconsistent with his character. However, he figured that if Shay couldn't understand where things had gone wrong, then she really wasn't worth the time it would take for him to offer an explanation.

Instead of walking away, Shay just stood there. It looked like she was waiting for further discussion or an invitation from him. Kylan just wasn't prepared to put any more energy towards Shay. Pierce sat awkwardly, waiting for Shay to take the hint and walk away. Finally, after a very pregnant pause, the server arrived with their drinks.

"Well, Shay, it was nice seeing you. We're just going to drink our martinis now. Enjoy your night," said Pierce pointedly.

She looked at Kylan, shooting daggers with her glare before she finally pivoted and walked away.

"That woman never gives up, does she?" Pierce chuckled. "Man, Shay is too desperate, even for me."

"Tell me about it," said Kylan, savoring the briny taste of his martini. Looking across the bar, a woman caught his eye. She looked familiar to him, but he couldn't quite place her. She and her friend were very nicely put together, and they were dressed less provocatively than most of the other women there. He couldn't take his eyes off the tall, Black woman wearing a pale blue silk slip dress and stiletto-heeled nude sandals. She was demurely sexy yet innocently cute at the same time. It took him a minute, then he had his smack my forehead moment when it dawned on him that she was the woman from The Elevated World. He decided to meet her tonight–no ifs, ands, or buts.

Dancing Queens

WHEN THEY ARRIVED AT SKYBAR, Indi and Gisselle each ordered a glass of rosé prosecco. They stood by the tall bar and surveyed the scene. It was a comfortably warm California evening, and the setting sun cast an orangey-pink glow that seemed to impart a sense of magic. The music pumping from the DJ booth was loud enough to dance, but it wasn't drowning out their voices; instead, the sound just seemed to carry itself away into the open sky. The atmosphere was just the vibe they were looking for.

"Santé," said Gisselle, with a smile on her face.

"Cheers, babe," Indi answered, clinking her best friend's glass before each woman took a sip. "This bubbly is delicious. It's exactly what I needed to give my heart a little lift." Indi had changed into a tasteful pale gold sequin romper, layered a few delicate chain necklaces, and put on high-heeled gold gladiator sandals. She may have been falling apart on the inside, but she appeared coolly confident to anyone who looked at her.

"You're so smart, beautiful, and fun, Indi. I know that the right man is out there for you. We just need to have faith,"

Gisselle squeezed her friend's hand. She hoped that her positive words would elevate her friend's mood. At age twenty-six, two years was a long time to invest in a failed relationship. On the outside, Indi looked like a tough little cookie, as if nothing would faze her, but clearly, Nathan's departure had really rattled her. She found it totally disrespectful, the way he had cheated on her friend so publicly. Gisselle wasn't convinced that Indi thought Nathan would be her happily ever after. Still, she understood that feeling of just being gutted when you think you're safe in a relationship, then having the rug suddenly pulled out from under you.

"To hell with Nathan," Indi managed to get the words out, but her voice was just a little bit shaky. "Maybe I'll just have to find a new boyfriend here tonight. On to bigger and better things, right? Definitely bigger, anyway."

"Touché," Gisselle said with a wink.

"In fact, I think we need to drink up, and hit the dance floor, then drink some more," said Indi, as she swallowed the last of her prosecco. "What do you say, babe?"

"You know I'm not much into dancing anymore," Gisselle demurred. "How about if we just order another glass?"

"No way, sister," Indi was determined to have a good time, which meant convincing her friend to join her on the dance floor. When Gisselle still didn't budge, she let her tone get a bit more serious. "Listen, Elle, I've really had a shit day. I know you didn't take Nathan very seriously, but I did. When I heard he got the series in New York, I stupidly believed that he would ask me to move out there with him. I didn't expect a marriage proposal, but I certainly didn't anticipate getting dumped, then for him to add insult to injury by fucking some bimbo in a restaurant. If ever there was a night I needed to rule the dance floor, it would be tonight, and I need my best friend to do it with me."

Gisselle looked into her friend's big, sad, watery brown eyes and gave her a little hug. She knew what she had to do. Turning to the hot Latino bartender, she said, "Four blow jobs, please."

He gave the women a sexy smile as he winked, flexed his pecs, and said, "Four blow jobs, coming right up!"

As he prepared their shots, carefully topping each glass with whipping cream, Indi said, "Yes, Gisselle, this is just what I needed tonight. The real thing would be better, but this is a reasonable facsimile."

"Okay," she replied, "Let's see if I even remember how to do this." Gisselle held her long, thick, curly black hair behind her as she carefully bent her face toward the shot glass.

"Because you can't use your hands," Indi reminded her, giggling. "You need to fit your whole mouth around the shot glass, pull it up with your lips and just toss it back."

"I know, girl. I was in a sorority. I can do this," Gisselle had to psych herself up a little.

"Whatever, you're too slow. I'm going first," Indi bent over the bar, picked up the shot in her mouth, and tossed it back, swallowing the whole thing in one gulp. A little bit of liqueur trickled out of one side of her lips. "Oops," she said when she noticed it, then dabbed it with a cocktail napkin. "Now it's your turn," she told Gisselle.

Although she hadn't done shots in a while, let alone a blow job shot, Gisselle would be a good sport tonight and get the job done. Besides, she was having fun, and it was totally harmless. She tossed one shot back, and some of hers dripped down her chin afterward. "Okay, Indi, the next one, no mess. Together, on the count of three. One, two, three, and down." They each took their second shot, and this time they swallowed neatly.

"That's what was called for. Alright, Indi, now I'm ready

to hit the dance floor," she said. Laughing, Gisselle took her friend's hand and made their way to the dance floor together. Tonight was 80s night, and the DJ was doing a great job of mixing. Many people were dancing, and the lights from the disco ball were refracting off the pool's surface, making every-thing feel just a bit more glamorous than your typical bar scene. It was fun to sway in this open-air atmosphere, where tourists mixed with locals, and celebrities blended in with the rest of the upscale, under forty crowd.

Both women adored 80s music because who doesn't love simple nostalgia? They danced conservatively at first, singing along timidly to Tiffany and Janet Jackson, then giggling as they got into the groove with Madonna and just had fun moving to Cyndi Lauper and classic ABBA. When Michael Jackson's Thriller played, Gisselle and Indi looked at each other and grinned with mischief. They recalled the Thriller line dance scene led by Jennifer Garner in the movie 13 Going on 30. They nodded in agreement and just went for it–together. The now not-so-sober besties led the Thriller routine across the dance floor. Moving rhythmically to the music, in perfect synchronicity. It didn't take long for the other Skybar patrons to join in on the fun.

By now, they had attracted everyone's attention, especially Kylan and Pierce, who was watching them with interest. Usually, that kind of attention-getting antic would be a red flag and a total turnoff for Kylan. Still, he just couldn't help himself–he was utterly transfixed by the woman he believed to be Gisselle Phillips, wearing the pale blue slip dress, dancing up a storm with the woman in the gold sequin romper. They looked like they were having the best time together, and nothing else mattered at that moment other than simple fun. Kylan thought there was something beautiful about a woman who had the self-confidence to just go out and have a simple good time.

Gisselle and Indi left the dance floor giggling when the song was over. As they started looking for a table, Indi saw that some of her friends from work had come in.

"Gisselle, I see some of the cast and crew from my show. Come over and let me introduce you," Indi said, seemingly in a more upbeat mood.

Gisselle shook her head. "That sounds like fun, but I'm really beat. Do you mind if I go home now that you have your people here?"

"You're my people, Elle, but I'll be fine now, and you can go home. Don't worry about me. I love you. Thank you for being with me tonight," Indi hugged her friend, then made her way over to her friends from the show.

Gisselle's eyes panned across Skybar one last time before she turned to leave. She caught her breath for a moment, and her gaze returned to a cocktail table where two thirtyish African American men were seated together, drinking classic martinis. They were dressed in fashionable suits, and she felt like one of them was watching her. She shook her head gently, thinking that she must be imagining things, then got into the elevator and rode down to street level.

"Pierce, that's her. She just left. I have to go." Pierce didn't even have time to respond. Kylan had already hopped off his stool and was walking away from the table. Singularly focused on following the willowy beauty in the silky, pale blue dress. Kylan hurriedly texted his driver to meet him downstairs, then followed Gisselle toward the door. He took the next elevator, and when he got out, he could hear her heels clicking on the marble floor as she walked toward the main doors to go outside. Just as she was about to get into a taxi, Kylan called out, "Wait–please wait just a minute. Miss! You forgot something."

All he could see were Gisselle's beautiful long legs

extending out from the rear passenger side of the taxicab. Then she stepped back out onto the sidewalk.

She looked at Kylan and recognized him as the man who had been staring at her upstairs at Skybar. "You said I forgot something?" she asked him.

Kylan hadn't planned that far in advance. He had grown adept at business talk but still found himself incredibly shy around women he liked. At this particular moment, he was at a loss for words.

"The meter's running, lady," they both heard the taxi driver call out.

Finally, Kylan said, "You forgot to give me your number."

Gisselle just looked at him for a moment, and they both laughed. "Oh my God, that's a terrible line. Are you kidding me?"

"Please let the taxi go. My driver has just pulled up," Kylan said as he gestured toward Atticus, who had just arrived.

Gisselle hesitated for a moment, then decided that her level of intrigue was too high to simply let this one go without further exploration. She sent the taxi away and introduced herself to Kylan.

"Hi, I'm Gisselle Phillips. It's nice to meet you," she began.

"And I'm Kylan Murray. I wanted to come to talk to you upstairs at Skybar, but then you were dancing, and next thing I knew, I saw you walking into the elevator," he explained.

"Ah, yes, the Thriller routine. I don't normally do that," Gisselle blushed as she was talking to him. "It's just that my friend had a rough day, and I was trying to encourage her to have a good time."

"Oh, it definitely looked like a good time," Kylan laughed gently. "I know this seems very forward, but I would like to get to know you better. I don't want to go back up to Skybar. Can I invite you to my place just to talk, maybe have some coffee, without a bunch of people watching?"

"Okay, Kylan, but we just met. Maybe you're new to LA, but it's generally not safe for women to get into a car and go home with a total stranger. Am I missing something?" Gisselle wanted to accept his invitation. Her intuition told her that Kylan was a regular guy, not a serial killer, but how could she be sure? Was it worth the risk?

"I know, but I promise I'm sane and totally harmless. I just don't want you to leave because I don't know if I'll ever find you again," he explained. Then he thought of something. "Are you on Twitter? Or LinkedIn? Instagram, even? Would you please look me up? And if that doesn't work, maybe my driver can vouch for me."

"Okay," Gisselle relented and pulled her phone out of her mini bag. "I'll look you up on LinkedIn, because that's the most reliable way to make sure you are who you say you are."

As she read Kylan's profile, Gisselle's eyes widened into saucers. Holy shit, she thought. This guy is major, as in he's practically a tycoon. What the hell? What does he want with me? The expression on her face must have given away her thoughts because Kylan laughed.

"Okay, Kylan Murray," she began, "What on Earth do you want with me?"

"You're fucking gorgeous," came his immediate response, "And I get the sense you are also brilliant and career-driven. Those are qualities that are hard to find in a person. Please allow me to take you to my home, where we will simply engage in enlightening conversation, get to know one another a little, and gauge our compatibility. Then my driver will take you home whenever you like."

As Kylan looked at her, he could tell she was still not convinced, and she wasn't answering him, so he sweetened the offer. "What about, if you come to my home tonight, I'll make a $500,000 donation to a charity of your choice in your name?"

"Well, I suppose it's for a good cause...." Gisselle said with a shy smile, her voice trailing off. She allowed Atticus to open the door of the limousine for her, and she climbed inside, her whole body tingling in anticipation of what this spontaneous adventure would bring.

Take Me Away to Malibu

THERE WASN'T much small talk during the drive. Thankfully, there was ample room between them in the spacious vehicle interior. Although Gisselle had placed her handbag to her left, they were careful to avoid resting their hands in the center. Kylan deliberately refrained from touching her because he didn't want to creep her out. He could tell that she was skeptical, as she should be, and he wanted her to know that he had no intention of molesting her or worse. He didn't want to scare her while driving west along the Pacific Coast Highway.

Almost an hour later, Atticus pulled up in front of Kylan's sprawling home along the coast of Malibu. Even though it was dark outside, this was an area that Gisselle knew well. She had grown up in Malibu, only a few doors down along the PCH from where Kylan appeared to reside. Her parents still lived there, so Gisselle knew that if she had to make a quick exit, she at least had somewhere safe to go. She had never just gone home with a stranger before. Even though she found Kylan to be ridiculously good-looking, the conservative person inside of her was chastising her reckless side for having put herself in such a vulnerable position. Hopefully, everything would be okay, and she wouldn't have to look back upon this night with regret.

As she stepped outside the vehicle, she took in the imposing white structure against the backdrop of the calm ocean. She immediately recognized it as a new home. In fact, whenever she had visited her parents during its construction, they had all discussed who the owner might be. Her parents had thought it might be an established movie star, but since Gisselle wasn't there all the time, she had never found out who the owner was. Now, she could let her parents know that the person who built this magnificent, sprawling beach house was Kylan Murray, entrepreneur extraordinaire.

Not sure what to do next, Gisselle stood on the driveway, staring at the house, studying its clean rooflines, and inhaling sharply. She hoped she hadn't just unwittingly hired herself out tonight as an escort. She didn't usually sleep with men on the first date (and this wasn't even a date). She was not a prude because she had dated a lot. She slept with dozens of guys, sometimes in casual hookups, and had been involved in a few serious relationships. She didn't usually meet them outside a bar, then ride straight home with them to have sex. Not that she wouldn't have sex with Kylan. Her mood was different; this wasn't how she envisioned her next relationship (or even non-relationship) starting. She had to say, it felt a little weird. She was hopeful that Kylan could figure out some ice-breaker to lighten the mood.

"Please follow me, my lady," Kylan said playfully as he ushered her inside the front door.

"Why, thank you," replied Gisselle, in a mock Southern Belle accent. Desperately nervous, she willed herself not to perspire and give away her anxiety. She didn't want Kylan to notice her discomfort, but it was a really weird thing to be inside a strange man's home late at night when there appeared to be no staff present. She thought he must at least have a housekeeper, but no one else was in sight. It seemed as though they were alone there. She was happy that she had limited her alcohol consumption that night, so she was aware of what was happening around her. Her behavior hadn't devolved into silliness.

"Are you okay?" he asked her.

She paused for a moment before answering. "Yes, Kylan, I'm fine. I'm just waiting for you to make your donation so that I can go home."

"Pardon me?" Kylan was a little taken aback.

"That was our deal, remember?" she responded. "You said that if I came to your home tonight, you would donate $500,000 to a charitable organization of my choosing, correct? So here I am, waiting for my donation in your home." She tried to keep her tone light, but her voice was slightly shaky.

"That is true," he conceded. He reached for his iPad on a nearby table and opened the internet search engine. "Please tell me, where would you like me to make my pledge?" He was sure that he knew the answer, even though Gisselle hadn't yet told him where she worked. He didn't want to startle her by letting her know he had seen her photo online, affiliated with The Elevated World, so he said nothing. He would wait for her to tell him about her career.

"Well, I work for a Los Angeles non-governmental organization that relies on charitable donations to maintain its operating budget. Our goal is to provide literacy support and reading materials to underprivileged youth. It's called The Elevated World. Any chance you'd be interested in making a donation there?" she asked him.

Kylan didn't know if it would impress Gisselle that earlier that day, he had already contributed $2,000,000 to The Elevated World or if telling her about his previous donation would turn her off. She might think he was bragging, and he didn't want to give her the impression that he was high on himself, so he decided to keep quiet about that. Besides, she would find out anyway since she was the organization's director.

"Yes, actually, I was looking it up earlier today. Someone, I know recently attended an Elevated World gala fundraising event and he was really impressed. You don't have to convince me," he told her.

Still, in a mild state of disbelief, Gisselle watched as Kylan made a $500,000 pledge. For donations of that amount, her major gifts officer would have to contact him the following week to complete the transaction and to ask him what kind of recognition he would like to receive. Now that Kylan had followed through on his end of the bargain, she was a bit nervous about her next steps. She wondered if she should stay a while and actually get to know him a little bit or if she should get out of there immediately.

"Thank you for doing that," she said, trying to be cool. "You're a very generous man."

"What can I say?" he responded as confidently as he could. "When I believe in something, I go all in." There was a gleam in his eye, and Gisselle couldn't tell yet if she thought he was cool and sexy or if he was a total nerd with no clue about how to meet women. "Now tell me," he continued. "Would you like for my driver to take you home now? Or would you care to stay for a little visit? I would love to give you a tour of my home and hear a little bit about you."

Biting her lower lip, Gisselle paused before she answered him. Part of her wanted to stay, and the other part feared where it could lead if she didn't go home right away. She didn't know anything about this guy. Kylan brought women home from Skybar every Friday night for all she knew. However, her curiosity got the better of her. She hadn't ever dated anyone like him before, a self-made man who could write a half-million dollar check on a whim. Maybe if there was no chemistry, he would be just a really good friend. On the other hand, if things heated up, who knew where it could eventually lead.

"Thank you, yes, I would love a tour," she finally breathed.

"Great," Kylan beamed at her. "But first, can I offer you anything to drink? Maybe sparkling water with a twist of lemon?"

"That's exactly what I crave right now, after all that dancing. Yes, please," Gisselle was relieved that he wasn't trying to ply her with alcohol.

"Follow me this way into the kitchen," he said casually.

As Gisselle followed Kylan into his spacious, modern chef's kitchen, which had a long wall of windows that faced the ocean, she was trying to conceal her awe. She was impressed with the tastefully functional layout and the long table that ran parallel to the windows. He must entertain friends here, she thought to herself. Of course, he must use a chef. Between the windows and the back wall of cabinetry, which also housed the appliances, was a huge island that Gisselle thought would be a great space to roll out pie crusts or cookie dough. She wondered what it would feel like to wake up every morning, listening to the waves crashing on the beach below and feeling the warmth of the sunshine just beaming down through the windows. Of course, her parents' house down the street was also magnificent. It had been built in the 1970s and needed some updating–it was nothing like this. Even her house in Hancock Park was impressive by most peoples' standards, but Kylan's place was palatial.

First, Kylan washed his hands, opened the fridge, and poured her a tall glass of sparkling water. Then he took a lemon from the decorative fruit bowl at the island's center and sliced it into perfect rounds, which he then used to garnish her drink.

"Fancy," she said with a grin.

"Only the best for you," came his playful reply.

They just stared at each other for a few moments, then they burst out laughing and had their drinks.

"You said you don't usually dance like that," he observed, "were you and your friend celebrating something?"

"Not celebrating exactly," she explained, "but my friend just broke up with somebody, so I was trying to cheer her up. How about you?'

"Well, tomorrow is my 32nd birthday, actually," said Kylan sheepishly.

"Awww, I guess tomorrow you have plans?" she asked.

"Not especially, nothing yet anyway," he was trying so hard not to blush.

"I'm ready for my house tour now, if you're still up for it," ventured Gisselle. She was feeling more confident now and a bit safer around him.

"Fantastic," Kylan said, putting down his glass. "Follow me."

Gisselle followed him through room after room. On the main level was the living area. Complete with a foyer, the massive kitchen where the tour began, a large modern living room, a casual den, Kylan's home office, and a full bathroom. The staircases were all open so that the sunlight could come right through into all rooms of the house. Below, Kylan showed her the master suite, plus three additional bedrooms, all with en suites and walk-in closets. Finally, a walk-out basement led directly to the beach, with a great room for entertaining. Another guest room with an en suite, another full bathroom, and most interestingly, a library and reading room, all tucked away. They had spent quite a bit of time in Kylan's library, where Gisselle couldn't help but take books off the shelves. She was curious about his taste in literature, and she could tell that these volumes had actually been opened and presumably read. Outside, facing the ocean, each level boasted a beautiful terrace with an open winding staircase to travel between floors.

Kylan had obviously used an architect who knew how to design a tasteful, timeless beach house that would eventually work for both a bachelor and a family. His interior design choices were also sound, noted Gisselle. She liked the soft color scheme of cloud white, pale wood tones, and splashes of blue and taupe that tied everything together. Usually, when she saw a man's home, the decor was sparse and uncomfortable, not to mention the typical man's dreary grays and blacks. On the other hand, Kylan seemed to appreciate soft touches in his furnishings, and the muted hues imparted a feeling of calm throughout the space.

"What do you think of my art collection?" he asked her.

"I really like your pieces," commented Gisselle, "but what I absolutely adore is your library. Thank you for letting me touch all your books. I'm very impressed with your collection of titles. There are more than just books about how to get ahead in business. You have a ton of classic fiction, new work, and biographies. I'm shocked. I don't normally meet men who read."

"You're kidding me," he replied. "My parents were both teachers, so I come by my love of reading, honestly. From the moment I learned to read for myself, I understood how a good book can transport you to another time and place, and you can be anyone. There are no limits with books. Your imagination just comes alive. Reading is what enabled me to find success in school and in life generally. I'm guessing you're a big reader too, or else you would have walked out of my library by now."

"Actually, I am," she confessed, "and that charity you just donated to, that's where I work. I'm a social worker and recently became the director of The Elevated World."

"I figured as much," he said sheepishly. "Actually, I thought it was you because I follow the organization on Twitter, and there was a post with your picture." He blushed. "I hope you don't mind that I noticed you at Skybar, and I was pretty sure that you were the woman in the picture."

"And you waited this long to tell me that?" she pretended to be offended and gave him a flirtatious smile.

The library was one of the smaller rooms in the house, and it felt pretty cozy. They were standing inches away from one another, their bodies in close proximity. Gisselle had removed her high heels at the front door, and barefoot she was just a few inches shorter than Kylan. She couldn't help but look up at him and notice that they were an ideal natural kissing height. Kylan must have noticed that at the exact same time because he leaned in for a kiss, but she playfully dodged him.

Taking his hand, she teasingly said, "Take me back upstairs and show me your Picasso."

Kylan dutifully obliged, then tried again to kiss her in front of the Picasso on the living room wall. Again, she artfully moved out of reach.

"Now, take me back to the Rodin," she cooed as she laced her fingers through his.

Once again, Kylan gently led her to the Rodin sculpture in his front entry hall. Yet again, he attempted a kiss, and she demurred.

"It's getting late," Kylan said, pointing out that it was now well past midnight. "Would you like my driver to take you home, or shall I show you to a guest room?"

Now it was Gisselle's turn to attempt a kiss, which she did, and Kylan responded decidedly well. He leaned down to meet her lips, and his kiss was tentative at first, then just a little bit deeper. His lips were full and firm. She liked how he gently placed his hands on her cheek and the other at the nape of her neck. He knew how to give a good kiss.

After a few moments, their lips parted, and Gisselle said, "Guest room, please."

Kylan quietly led her into a guest room next door to the master suite. He showed her where the towels were and offered her a clean robe and slippers. Gisselle felt like she was in a hotel. He even offered her a charger for her phone. I could get used to this, she thought to herself.

"Goodnight, Kylan, and thank you," she said.

"Sweet dreams, Gisselle. Thank you for coming home tonight," his voice sounded husky now as he turned and walked away to his own room.

Damn, thought Gisselle. Maybe I should have gone home, or maybe I should have invited him to spend the night here with me. Decisions, decisions...

Happy Birthday

THE FOLLOWING MORNING, Kylan awoke to the aroma of food wafting down to him from the kitchen. Usually, he set his alarm to wake him up at 7:00 a.m., even on Saturday, because he liked to keep himself on a routine. His typical weekend morning usually involved waking up early, having a light, quick bite, then going for a run oceanside before it got too hot outside. Then he would come home, take a swim in the ocean, and come inside for a shower and steam, then carry on with business. Kylan enjoyed his days outside the office, but business was always in the back of his mind. He sometimes wondered what it was that other people did during their leisure time. As much as he liked to go out with friends and business colleagues, it was a relief to him when he could just stay home and chill. Tonight, for example, was his birthday, and he hadn't really wanted to make any plans, but Pierce had insisted.

Meeting Gisselle last night had entirely made up for the unpleasantness of being tortured by Shay. He had really dodged a bullet there. He hoped to God that he wouldn't constantly be subjected to the stereotypical gold digger. Most of his business associates were married, and their wives were normal. Some carried on with their careers, while others were stay-at-home moms, but they were nothing like Shay. He wondered how it had come to be that his associates could attract intelligent women when all he could seem to find were social-climbing Shay types. Yes, she looked like a hot little Black blow-up doll come to life, but she had turned out, in essence, to be filled with hot air. Shay had no shame, and Kylan could probably keep sleeping with her just for fun, but he had outgrown her type. He needed a real partner with education, ethics, values, and a strong sense of self-worth–someone like Gisselle.

Of course, his best friend Pierce had worked so diligently in medical school to complete his specialty in ophthalmology, and to finally collect the big paychecks after years of a meager resident salary, that all he wanted to do now was have some fun. While Kylan certainly didn't begrudge him that, he felt it was time for him to move on from the Shay types. It's not that he wanted to start a committed relationship right away. Still, he felt that at this stage of his life, he at least wanted to be in a relationship with a quality person that could potentially lead to a long-term commitment, eventually.

Kylan hesitated before getting out of bed, wondering what the etiquette was for the morning after, when a woman had spent the night in a guest room. Should he look in on her and see if she was still asleep or needed anything? Should he wake her up or let her sleep in if she was still asleep? Maybe he should start breakfast or wait until she had woken up so he could ask her what her preference was. He decided to just wake up, subtly look in on Gisselle, then go up to the kitchen and make coffee. Then he snapped out of his daydream and remembered that the smell of breakfast had already woken him up.

He jumped out of bed and padded down the hall to look

into the guest room where Gisselle had spent the night. She wasn't there. The bed was perfectly made, and there was no sign of her belongings. He realized that she must be upstairs right now, making breakfast for him. He was a bit embarrassed because, as the host, he should have woken up earlier to make sure that he could prepare breakfast for her, not the other way around.

Expecting to find Gisselle in his kitchen, he was shocked to see no sign of her. What he did notice, however, was a place setting at the head of the table, properly laid out, with a homemade cinnamon bun on the plate and a bowl of fresh raspberries to the left. The coffee maker was brewing. He looked around again, expecting her to walk in, but he felt distinctly alone. On the vast kitchen island, she had left him a small cake and written "Happy Birthday Kylan" across the top, in perfectly piped icing. Next to the cake, she *had written him a note. It read:*

"Dear Kylan, I wish you the happiest birthdays. Thank you for your hospitality last night and generous gift to the Elevated World. Best, Gisselle."

Ouch! He thought to himself. Was this the ultimate kiss-off? Shit! Shit! Shit! She hadn't even left her number. Forget a Harvard Business School MBA refresher course on microeconomics–he needed a course on how to get and keep a good woman.

Although he wasn't particularly impressed with her departure, he thought that it might be a good sign if she had felt comfortable enough to hunt around inside his kitchen, looking for baking ingredients. If she had really wanted to ditch him, she would have simply woken up and left. She wouldn't have spent time in his kitchen, facing the apparent chance that he would wake up to join her. The evidence in his recycle bin told him she hadn't baked from scratch. He saw the empty Pillsbury Cinnamon Roll package and the Betty

Crocker confetti cake mix. Nevertheless, she had been up at the crack of dawn to do this for him and remembered his birthday.

Unfortunately, she hadn't left her phone number or other potential contact information. He knew where she worked, but he didn't feel it would be appropriate to contact her there, not yet anyway. Surely, she wouldn't have gone through all this trouble. Baking him the cake, making him breakfast, if she didn't like him. She had to at least feel a little warmth toward him if she remembered that today was his birthday.

His thoughts were interrupted by a text from Pierce inquiring how lucky he had gotten the night before. He chose not to answer the question but instead called his friend.

"Pierce, my man, you're up so early texting me. Did you even go to sleep last night?" he asked.

"Well, there may have been a little sleep involved, but my little honey from last night tasted so sweet...." Pierce would have gone on, but Kylan interrupted him.

"Please tell me that Shay just left you alone after I left," Kylan said, concerned that his ex might be trying to land his best friend as a revenge tactic.

"No way, man! I brought home a cute little female, the one dancing with your girl, the sexy white girl in sequins. She has energy to burn, that one!" Pierce enthused.

"Okay, you know she was out last night on the rebound, right? Gisselle told me that her best friend just broke up with someone, and they went to Skybar to cheer her up, Kylan told him.

"And? Do you have a problem with a girl with a broken heart? Let me tell you who can heal a broken heart, brother—Dr. Pierce James doesn't just fix your eyes, man. He can heal your heart too." Kylan burst out laughing when he heard Pierce say this. He was so childish and yet so lovable at the same time.

"Did you get her name, at least?" Kylan asked him. "Because at least I got the name of my honey: Gisselle Phillips."

"You know how to make a brother feel small, don't you," Pierce pretended to be insulted. "Yes, I got a name. Mine is called Indi Priest, and I'm telling you, man, she made me want to get down on my knees and pray."

"Okay, stop, time out, TMI," began Kylan. "Let's talk about the plan for later. You know I'm having an early dinner with my parents tonight. Do you want me to swing by and pick you up on the way to the Chateau Marmont?"

"Yes, thanks, that would be perfect," Pierce responded.

"Right, I'll text you when I'm on my way," Kylan confirmed. Then he added, "Wait, Pierce, did Indi give you her phone number by any chance?"

"Hmm, we weren't too focused on exchanging digits. There was plenty of digital penetration and exchanging of bodily fluids, but no trading telephone numbers, my friend." Pierce had never been shy about boasting of his sexual exploits.

"I said no TMI, please, no more," Kylan mock pleaded. "I'm asking you because it was the strangest thing this morning. Gisselle slept in the guest room–"

"Boo!" Pierce interrupted him. "What is with you and the guest room? Are you kidding me?"

"As I was saying," Kylan resumed his train of thought, "Gisselle woke up super early this morning, went into my kitchen to bake me cinnamon buns and a birthday cake, then she left before I woke up today. She went to all that trouble, set the breakfast table and everything, then just left. No phone number, no social media handle, nothing. She just vanished before I woke up. I don't get it."

"Oh, this honey's playing hard to get," ventured Pierce. "She ain't going to make this easy for you. It's simpler for you to buy a new company than to find a new girlfriend, brother. What is wrong with you?"

"It's not funny, bro. I like Gisselle. I even gave her charity a $500,000 pledge," Kylan explained.

"Wait a minute," said Pierce, a little bit stunned. "You mean to tell me that even a half million dollar donation and behaving like a gentleman with your guest room and everything wasn't enough to get that woman's phone number?"

"That's right," signed Kylan.

"Shit, brother, this one's going to make you work for it," Kylan could practically hear Pierce shaking his head in resignation as he spoke the words.

"Don't I know it," agreed Kylan.

"Where have you been?" Indi practically screamed as she knocked impatiently at Gisselle's front door. She opened it, wearing her robe, and gestured an invitation to her friend to come inside.

"What do you mean, where have I been," Gisselle replied. "You know exactly where I've been. I went to Skybar with you last night, and now I'm at home, and as you can see, I just got out of the shower."

"I've been concerned about you because I know that you left the club before I did last night, and yet you seem to have arrived home after me," Indi began. "Therefore, there are several hours between your departure from Skybar and your return home, which you have yet to account for. Have you not seen any of my texts? I've been worried sick."

"No, Indi, I turned off my phone last night on purpose," Gisselle explained. "I met someone, he took me out to his Malibu mansion, and I stayed the night. I just got home a little while ago."

"Excuse me?" Indi burst out. "Did I just hear you say that you met someone, and he drove you out to Malibu last night? As in, you rode in a stranger's car–"

"Limo," interrupted Gisselle. "He asked if he could take me to his home in Malibu in his chauffeured limo. And he made a $500,000 donation to The Elevated World, simply because I agreed to come home with him."

"And that didn't creep you out a little?" she asked, appearing concerned. "I mean, it's nice that he has big money and everything, but what do you know about this guy?"

Gisselle licked her lips, remembering their kiss. "I know enough," she began, deciding not to tell Indi about his library at the risk of sounding schmaltzy. "Let's just say we may have a few things in common, but at the end of the day, he's probably just your typical obnoxious tech billionaire."

"Well, are you going to see him again?" she queried.

"Hmm, I don't think so," Gisselle replied, but as the words came out of her mouth, she thought that she probably should have left him her phone number in the note. In fact, she wished she had left him her number. Instead, she had fled the moment that she heard him stir. Why was she always doing this? Why couldn't she just relax and allow herself to be swept off her feet? Because fairy tales don't happen in real life, she thought to herself, which is why we call them fairy tales. "Tell me about how your night turned out," she continued. "Did you have a nice time with your people from the show?

"Did I have a nice time?" Indi licked her lips for emphasis. "If you're asking me if I achieved my goal of getting some dick last night, the answer is yes, my friend. I did, in fact, get some delicious dick from a very hot doctor, and I've completely gotten over what's-his-name. I love going to a rooftop bar above a fancy hotel. It makes it so convenient to just get a room and hook up."

"Well then," said Gisselle, "I guess you could say that's mission accomplished."

"Abso-fucking-lutely," Indi agreed with a wink. "Now, I have to say that I actually think this is the point where things could get interesting. We're going out again tonight: Chateau Marmont. You can't even argue with me because we're already on the guest list."

Gisselle laughed as she said goodbye to her friend, then went into the kitchen to make herself a late breakfast.

A NIGHT at the Chateau Marmont bar was always a treat. It was one of those places where actor types went, pretending they didn't want to be recognized, yet secretly hoping that someone would be there to photograph them. Gisselle smiled to herself, remembering her parents having gone there regularly when she was younger. In fact, they still went there from time to time. She knew that tonight her parents had plans to go out with some of her father's castmates from the soap and thought how cute it would be if she and Indi were to bump into them.

As she was getting dressed, thoughts of Kylan kept sneaking up on her. If she was so unimpressed by him and all his success, then how come she just couldn't get him out of her head? It made no sense. Gisselle wasn't looking for a man to take care of her, not at all. She had a career that she was proud of and had just begun her professional trajectory. Social workers were indeed notoriously underpaid, but Gisselle was passionate about the work that she did. She was proud to be the director of operations at The Elevated World. Her mission was to help the underprivileged children of Los Angeles improve their literacy and provide them with the proper support to do so. Besides, her grandmother had left her such a generous estate that she would be able to follow her dreams, as opposed to stressing out over her paycheck. For that, she would be eternally grateful.

Gisselle was trying to figure out what to wear. Tonight was a more upscale destination, with a more laid-back crowd than last night's adventure. She was considering wearing a fabulous cream-colored slim-cut pantsuit, with a silky camisole and sky-high heels, for that sleek, fashionable monochrome look that was currently so stylish. Or did she want to wear a slip dress again? Maybe tonight she could wear her terracotta silk maxi length slip dress, which was low cut in the back, with a high slit? She decided on the cream suit for tonight, and she accented her look with chunky gold accessories.

She styled her beautifully thick hair in its naturally curly Afro style. Her hair was an absolute gift. Gisselle loved having a healthy head of hair, and she took care to keep her tight curls well-moisturized to ensure elasticity and reduce breakage. Other women might take a different view, but Gisselle loved that her natural hairstyle made her look just a little bit wild. She viewed it as an extension of her self-expression. For a moment, she let herself remember the feel of Kylan's hands touching the back of her neck during their long, slow kiss. That touch had sent tingles all down Gisselle's spine.

As she continued getting ready, she asked herself whether she had perhaps opted to wear the pantsuit on the off-chance that she and Indi would run into Kylan and his friend again tonight. Then she did a reality check and chastised herself for being so silly. Of course, they weren't going to run into Kylan again tonight. Last night was a total one-off. Los Angeles was a big place, and what were the odds that they would both be going to the same location two nights in a row? Practically nil, she thought. And even if they were going to cross paths, did she seriously believe that wearing a suit on a Saturday night would impress him? After all, tonight was an opportunity to make a fashion statement, not get ahead in business.

If she were Kylan, living in that magnificent home in Malibu, she thought there would be practically no reason to ever leave. And speaking of leaving, Gisselle wondered if she had made the right choice when she pulled her disappearing act this morning. Yes, Kylan had been extraordinarily polite and was a self-made man who liked to read. He read actual books, and he collected the classics. Whereas most men in his position would have built a home movie theater, Kylan had chosen to build a home library. Wasn't this her absolute dream partner?

She wondered whether Kylan had enjoyed his warm cinnamon buns this morning and if he had been turned on to find the birthday cake. Part of her regretted having left without a word this morning. She wished she had had the courage to leave her full name and number. Then her cynical side reminded her that she may have just been setting herself up for disappointment. Kylan probably had women falling all over themselves, trying to get close to him. After all, he was quite a catch. Besides, he knew where she worked, and if he wanted to, he could easily find a way to contact her through The Elevated World.

Just as Gisselle was fastening her vintage gold watch around her delicate wrist, she heard the doorbell ring. She came to the front entrance to find her friend wearing a very chic taupe-colored ensemble of high-waist belted vegan leather shorts, lace-edged camisole, and a fitted Moto jacket. Tonight, her shoe choice was little western-style dark beige suede booties. Indi was nothing if not well put together.

"Are you ready to go, gorgeous?" Indi asked her. "The taxi is outside waiting for us."

"Yes, let me just grab my clutch and lock the door," replied Gisselle before stepping outside and locking up.

Pierce licked his lips as he surveyed the scene at the Chateau Marmont. He liked to play and was looking forward to another successful hunt. On weekdays, he typically worked a full clinic schedule. On top of that, he had been on call last week, which meant that he needed to have some serious fun this weekend to offset all the stress of the week before. Looking around, he noticed that Indi, his playmate from Skybar last night, was seated with her same beautiful friend in a cozy booth around the corner. From how she was sitting, her legs partially extending from the edge of the booth, he could admire her toned, shapely little legs. Pierce was of average height, and he liked petite women. He didn't usually date white girls, but he liked Indi's energy.

"Kylan," he said to his buddy, "is it my imagination, or is your cinnamon bun-cake-baking honey sitting over there, to the left? I do believe that both our honeys are here in this room tonight. What do you say, Kylan, shall we join them?"

"How can we join them? What if they already have plans? Maybe they're meeting people," Kylan objected. He shyly looked over at their table. Gisselle was so attractive, in a much understated kind of way, the total opposite of Shay. Today, Gisselle wore a cream-colored pantsuit that looked more like evening chic than office wear. The way she had styled her hair so naturally, she looked like a total bombshell. More specifically, she had a subtle elegance about her, a quiet kind of sexiness that Kylan found magnetic.

"I looked up my girl Indi on Facebook," began Pierce. "Her relationship status is still single, and I think she and your girl Gisselle are pretty much joined at the hip. They're not roommates, though, because their photos inside one another's homes look different. Indi is in the industry, she does hair and makeup, but Gisselle has a more normal job."

"I know,' Kylan said. "Gisselle works for a charity. She's that social worker whose picture I showed you, remember?"

"What are you saying, brother? Have you been stalking her or something? Do I need to call the *#metoo* movement and let them know that you're on the prowl?" teased Pierce.

"That's actually not funny, Pierce. Please don't call me a stalker," said Kylan in a serious tone. Pierce understood that he had misspoken and changed his facial expression right away. Kylan continued, "I was trying to maximize my charitable contributions for tax purposes. My financial advisor agreed that The Elevated World was a good cause and a worthy recipient. Afterward, I checked their Twitter feed to see what local events they were putting on, and that's when I saw Gisselle's picture. When she showed up at Skybar last night, I figured it was an opportunity to meet her. I like her. She's a smart, hard-working woman who also happens to be very attractive."

"Now that you got all that off your chest, brother, let's see what these birds say when we go on over and say hello," said Pierce, smiling as he rose from his seat. Feeling just a bit shy, Kylan took a deep breath, finished his drink, and followed him.

Indi looked up as the men approached the women's table and gave Pierce a welcoming smile. When Gisselle saw Kylan, she hesitated for a few seconds before gesturing for them to sit down.

"Hi again, ladies. How are you doing tonight," Kylan began. "My name is Kylan Murray," he said to Indi.

"Well, hello, Kylan, and I'm just fine, thank you for asking," replied Indi, "I've heard about you, and it's nice to meet you. Gisselle has told me some very nice things about you." Then, turning to Pierce, she said, "I didn't know that you were coming here tonight, handsome. So good to see you again."

Pierce sat next to Indi and started stroking her back while talking.

"Hi again, Kylan," began Gisselle, "I suppose I should wish you a happy birthday."

"Yes, I suppose you could," replied Kylan. "Or, you could have wished me a happy birthday this morning when you had the chance. You didn't even leave me your number."

"Well, it's lucky we met here tonight, isn't it?" Gisselle couldn't help it. She was flirting with Kylan. He was incredibly hot. There was no good reason she should deny herself the pleasure of that man's velvet kisses.

"I suppose so," agreed Kylan. "Can I order a bottle of champagne for the table?"

"That would be lovely," Indi thanked him.

A few minutes later, as the group was toasting their glasses of Perrier Jouet, Pierce shot Kylan a look that said, let's get out of here. Before he had even seen her, Kylan could sense her presence–Shay Armstrong was in the bar and walking decidedly towards their table.

"Kylan," Shay was anything but shy, and she had walked right up to their table to give Kylan a piece of her mind. "Why did you leave Skybar last night without saying goodbye to me? And why haven't I heard from you? You know I wanted to take you out for your birthday, and now I see you with another woman? Would you please explain to me what's happening here?" As she waited for her answer, Shay was drumming her long, pointy, hot pink lacquered fingernails on the table, making everyone uncomfortable.

"Please excuse me for just a moment," said Kylan, getting up from the table. He steered Shay a few feet away before speaking to her politely.

"Shay, I've made it clear to you that I'm not interested in

continuing our relationship. We're no longer friends. We're not dating anymore. I need you to back off. If you have any regard for me or my feelings, you'll respect my wishes."

From where Gisselle was seated, she could see Shay staring daggers at her before she pivoted on her five-inch tall stiletto heels and marched herself out of the Chateau Marmont bar.

Returning to the table, Kylan apologized for the interruption. "Please excuse what just happened. Shay and I dated a few times, then we ended things, and it looks like she's just taking some time to let it sink in."

"Maybe we can move this little party somewhere more private," suggested Pierce, nuzzling Indi's neck.

"How about if we all come to my place for one more round of champagne," offered Gisselle.

"That would be nice," Kylan answered right away.

"Sounds good to me," Pierce agreed.

"Perfect, that's a plan," Kylan said as he gestured to their server to pay their bill before the four of them left together in Kylan's chauffeured limousine.

Let's Get Comfortable

GISSELLE WAS glad that she had remembered to tidy up. Unlike Kylan, she didn't have an entire staff at her beck and call. Yes, she had help with lawn care, but Gisselle had grown accustomed to doing all the housekeeping herself. For now, that was manageable because she was living alone in the house and didn't have any pets. She figured it would be cruel to keep a pet, what with the long hours she worked. She would never be at home, able to spend any time with it, and any pet would get lonely. Come to think of it, even she found herself lonely in that big house from time to time. Well, she wouldn't be lonely tonight.

Kylan blew out as Atticus pulled the limousine up in front of Gisselle's stately home in Hancock Park. He had not expected that Gisselle would live in this kind of dwelling. Obviously, dating back to the 1920s, the home's architecture reflected the Art Deco style that had been so popular in Los Angeles at the time. Suppose you were a wealthy Los Angeleno a hundred years ago. In that case, you were either building a Tudor-style home, a Mediterranean villa, an English Country estate, or an Art Deco piece.

Sensing Kylan's surprise, Gisselle felt compelled to explain how it came to be that she, at age 26, owned a generously sized home in the wealthy suburb of Hancock Park. "This house belonged to my grandmother, the late Georgina Phillips, the trailblazing Black actress whose television and film career spanned decades. I'm her only grandchild, we were very close, and she left me most of her estate when she passed away."

"Wow, lucky you," said Pierce. Then he corrected himself, "I'm sorry that she died, but it was very generous of her to give you this property as a gift."

"It's okay, Pierce. I'm not offended," she assured him. "I knew what you meant."

"I'm sorry too, Gisselle," offered Kylan. "Does it make you feel still close to her to live in her house?"

"Absolutely, it does! I love living here," Gisselle enthused. "Ever since I was a little girl, I would spend my weekends with my grandmother, and I even moved in with her for my last couple years of college. She had the coolest outlook on life—she was definitely a pro-age woman—there were no limits on the kinds of things we used to do together. And she told the best stories about all her co-stars, her directors, the gentleman friends she had after my grandfather passed away."

"She was a very young widow," Indi interjected. "But Gisselle has left out the absolute best part of her life here in Hancock Park," she continued with a wink. "I'm her next-door neighbor."

"Is that so?" mused Pierce.

"Except that I live with my parents in the Tudor next door," Indi clarified, "in the guesthouse."

"Which is a little Tudor cottage larger than most people's actual homes." Gisselle laughed as they approached her front door, taking their time to cross the expansive front lawn. "My grandmother was wild. I can't wait to show you the fireplace mantle, which she had a bunch of her movie star friends sign at a party. Natalie Wood, James Dean, Marlon Brando, Elizabeth Taylor, Montgomery Clift, Sidney Poitier, Cary Grant, and Bing Crosby, to name a few. If you want, you can try and see who else's names you recognize."

"You've got to be kidding me," said Kylan, completely in awe. "Is there any chance she saved some of her old movie scripts? I would love to see those."

"Of course, you would ask me that question," Gisselle mused, remembering his penchant for reading. "You know, the study is full of bookshelves laden with scripts, some from movies and some from her television series, but I haven't looked at them in years. There's literally a whole wall of scripts in the study. If you remind me later, I can show them to you. I think she used to ask the weekly guest stars to sign her television scripts." Gisselle explained as she turned the key in the front door lock.

As she opened the door, Gisselle felt a little giddy with anticipation. Although this hadn't been part of the plan, Kylan was clearly very interested in her, despite her earlier disappearing act. She thought that maybe she should soften her stance about him because perhaps when an eligible bachelor literally has a billion dollars, which could make things very awkward regarding meeting women. If anything, Kylan's social impairment made him more attractive because it told her that he probably wasn't out every weekend trying to pick up new women. Although, she was slightly put off by that woman who had come to their table at the bar. Maybe she would ask Kylan about her later, or perhaps she wasn't important enough to worry about.

"Please come in, everyone," Gisselle said as she opened the door and ushered the group into her grand entrance hall. She knew that most people her age preferred sleek lines and spare decor. Still, Gisselle had always enjoyed more traditional, warmer finishings. Of course, Kylan's modern beach house design was spectacular by anyone's standards. Still, this old-fashioned Hollywood glamor look was more reflective of her traditional personal aesthetic. Her grandmother had taken great pride in maintaining the home's finishes and proper upkeep. Over the years, she had updated and renovated certain aspects of the kitchen and bathrooms. Still, overall the original feeling of the house remained intact.

"How about we sit in the living room?" she suggested.

Indi led the way, and everyone followed suit. The men went straight to the fireplace mantle, which, as Gisselle had described, had been autographed by many Old Hollywood stars. The wood mantle was painted a soft matte black, and everyone's signature appeared to be written in chalk. No one dared to touch the handwriting lest they actually left a smudge. Gisselle could tell they were wondering and said, "Yes, the autographs were all done in chalk. However, one of the set painters came over and applied a preservative, so it's there to stay. Otherwise, how would I be able to dust?"

The icebreaker worked, and both men chuckled. Indi took off her little Moto jacket, and Gisselle removed her blazer. Kylan looked over at her and admired her delicate collarbone, pretty shoulders, and how one camisole strap seemed to slip off just a little. Pierce had moved on from the autographed fireplace and examined all the old photographs on display, trying to guess who everyone was. It was a lot to take in for anyone who hadn't grown up in the industry.

"Guys, please sit down, make yourselves comfortable," said Gisselle. "How about I go to the kitchen and get us some glasses, and we can open a bottle of wine?"

"That sounds great, thank you," Kylan was just hoping that tonight, he might have the opportunity to kiss her again, which might lead to something more. He wasn't expecting a lot, just maybe her telephone number this time, now that he knew where she lived and worked. He couldn't understand the purpose of her disappearing act. He had enough experience playing cat and mouse games, and his encounter with Shay had taught him that it was better to be dating no one than to date the wrong person. He had to admit that he was relieved to see that Gisselle had her own money, so at least he had confidence that she wouldn't turn out to be a gold digger.

As soon as Gisselle left the room, Indi looked at Kylan and asked, "What is going on with that woman who came to our table? We left because of her, right?"

"We went out a few times, but it wasn't working out," Kylan was trying to be kind.

Pierce, however, preferred to be blunt: "That woman at Bar Marmont was Shay Armstrong. She's been after our Kylan for ages, just trying to rub up against him and, you know. So Kylan finally takes the bait and goes out with her a few times, then he sees her on Instagram Live vlogging about her five-point plan to land a rich man. Needless to say, Kylan was immediately repulsed and broke things off, but Shay apparently can't take a hint and move on."

"Well, at least you're not pretending to be subtle," Kylan said wryly.

"A brother gotta tell it like it is," Pierce laughed as he shook his head, "and if your friend Gisselle is concerned about Shay, you can assure her that there is nothing to worry about."

"That's good to know," Indi was relieved. "I'm going to go help Gisselle uncork that bottle," she said as she rose and walked off towards the kitchen.

Gisselle and Indi returned to the living room a couple of minutes later with a bottle each of red and white wine. Depositing everything atop the large coffee table in front of where everyone was sitting. The men drank the red, a Shiraz, while the women preferred the Chablis. They made small talk while they sipped their wine, and Gisselle couldn't help but notice that Pierce and Indi were getting very cozy. Looking over at Kylan, she wondered whether he would be expecting intimacy tonight or if he even knew what he wanted.

"Well," Kylan began, "I'm glad you told us about your late grandmother and how she left you the house and everything. Otherwise, I would have mistakenly thought that you were siphoning funds away from your charity."

"Moi?" gasped Gisselle in a mocking tone. She liked that Kylan had a sense of humor. "I would never, you know that."

"Would I, though? How would I know that?" Kylan challenged her. "I would have loved to have gotten to know you better, except that you ghosted me this morning."

"Roasted!" jeered Pierce. "Kylan, Gisselle didn't ghost you. She's here with you now." Then, turning to Gisselle, he said, "A good wingman needs to help his brother out."

Kylan realized he needed to get over it. He smiled sheepishly at Gisselle, saying, "You know, those were the tastiest cinnamon buns I've had in a long while. I enjoyed my birthday cake very much. So thank you."

"It was my pleasure," Gisselle replied flirtatiously.

"Now, I would have loved to have shared it with you this morning, but I'll happily settle for drinks tonight."

"I know what we should do," piped up Indi. "Let me get out the Scrabble board, and we can play sexy scrabble."

"Oh, no," Gisselle pretended to shake her head in embarrassment.

"Oh yes," said Indi, winking at Pierce. "We are going to only spell out dirty words. The winner gets a blow job shot, prepared lovingly by me."

They passed the time quickly, everyone giggling over, spelling out their dirty scrabble word choices. Surprisingly, the women came up with the most words. Gisselle figured that the men must have been holding back out of some sense of propriety. As they were wrapping up, she noticed that Pierce was whispering something in Indi's ear, and then he started nuzzling her neck, and his hand was moving up her thigh.

"Elle, thank you for a really fun night," Indi began, "but if you don't mind, I think Pierce and I shall retire next door to my parent's guest house, so if you don't mind making your own blow job...."

'Go ahead, Indi. Have fun, you too," Gisselle said with a wink. "It was nice meeting you, Pierce."

Gisselle got up and walked Indi and Pierce to the front door. After they left, she saw Kylan had tidied up the Scrabble board and was about to go.

"How about tonight, you stay in my guest room?" she asked him.

Kylan pretended to think about it before he smiled and said, "Alright, but now it's your turn to show me your library."

"I get it," she teased, "You show me yours, and I'll show you mine? Let me just turn off the lights downstairs, and then I'll take you up to the study and let you finger the scripts."

"I do like the sound of that...." Kylan couldn't resist.

A New Perspective

"You know, Gisselle, you're not the typical sort of woman I meet," Kylan began as she led him up a wide winding stone staircase. "I feel you possess a strong sense of compassion and empathy deep in your soul. Your chosen profession is so wildly different from what most attractive women in their late twenties would choose to do. I imagined you to be a little different for an independently wealthy person."

"What do you mean, like a little trustafarian? Going out to clubs every night, posting pictures of myself in my outfit of the day, pretending to be a social media influencer?" she laughed. "I've always had money, more than I ever needed. My parents actually live just a few houses away from you in Malibu. That's where I grew up. We might have met eventually, even if you hadn't followed me out of the Skybar last night."

"Interesting. How come you didn't mention that last night?" he asked. Then he continued, "It's just been my experience, and I know it sounds like an unfair stereotype. Women with money they didn't earn tend to have vapid personalities.

Their interest skews more toward tending to their social media accounts instead of working to improve society and give back, as it were."

"That's funny you should say that," she observed. "I'd never thought compassion had anything to do with material possessions. We simply are who we are, whether we have little money or a lot. The drive to help others, and our capacity for empathy, doesn't fluctuate like an interest rate. You're either the type of person who strives to make a difference in the world, or you're not."

"Would you say that a person's worldview can change, depending on their circumstances?" he asked.

"I'm not sure," Gisselle was thinking about her answer. "I would say that your outward appearance can change, and a person can alter themselves superficially. You either have a heart that wants to share, or you don't. You could try and impress someone by taking on a particular cause. Still, your true colors will eventually come through if your heart and mind aren't devoted. I like to surround myself with friends who display their authentic selves. How about you?"

"I believe it was Hamlet who said to 'assume a virtue if you have it not—am I right?" Kylan was obviously trying to impress her.

"I like a man who knows his Shakespeare," she said softly. "Although, I think he meant there was that, if a person has no innate virtues, they don't need to pretend to adopt one. Rather, they're supposed to find a cause, or a belief, that truly resonates with them, that brings meaning to their life, a kind of purpose. What are your thoughts on that?"

Instead of answering her with words, when they reached the top of the stairs, Kylan gently took Gisselle's hand. Gazing into her big, dark brown eyes, he brought her fingers to his lips and kissed them. When she didn't pull away, he wrapped his arms around her and drew her in for a kiss. As he tilted his face down to kiss her, he noted they were just the perfect height for one another. His lips were hot, and he kissed her gently at first, then more urgently. She liked his taste, the gentle contact of his lips pressing down on hers. As his confidence in their kiss grew, he let his tongue explore her mouth as their kiss deepened.

Neither one of them knew where this exploratory kiss would lead, and neither wanted to be the first to pull away. Gisselle let her hands travel over his shirt, across his lower back, then up towards his shoulders. Through the fabric of his clothing, she could feel his strong musculature, firm beneath her touch. His shoulders were just broad enough, and moving her hands back down his torso, she could appreciate how his waist narrowed into a healthy vee shape. She liked that he kept himself in good shape without overdoing it. Gisselle was always suspicious of men who spent too much time getting overbuilt at the gym. On the other hand, Kylan spent most of his time in the office and just enough time keeping fit. Balance was key.

Eventually, Kylan lifted his lips up off of hers. He didn't want to pull away, but he knew he had to, or he would get to the point of no return. Gisselle could tell precisely what he was thinking as she looked up at him. "Hmm," she cooed, her voice teasing him, "the study is just down this hall. I know you're dying to see those vintage scripts."

"The scripts. Yes, the scripts," Kylan had been so engrossed in their kiss that he had practically forgotten about Gisselle's grandmother's old scripts.

The wall sconces bathed the upstairs hallway in a romantic, golden glow. With high, coved ceilings, he felt like he was in another world with Gisselle, a calm and happy place that no one could disturb. Kylan could almost imagine himself on a movie set, playing the part of the male romantic hero in Gisselle's life story. At the end of the hall, Gisselle led him into a large, airy study with glass-paned French doors that opened out onto a spacious balcony. Through the glass, in the darkness of the night outside, Kylan could make out the outlines of topiaries and elegant outdoor furniture. This Old Hollywood oasis made his own private library look like a cave.

She flicked on the lights, then demonstrated how to safely slide open the glass cabinetry that protected the bookshelves from dust. "Please feel free to take them off the shelves and look at them. Just place them back carefully, as you found them."

"Wow," he said, impressed. "So this is your library of vintage Hollywood scripts. I'm almost at a loss for words. Did your grandmother used to read lines in here too?"

"Yes, actually, from time to time, she would play out her scenes with her co-stars right in this very room. Unfortunately, I was too young at the time to understand or appreciate the kind of talent that she had. Like, I was aware that she was a famous actress, and I knew she was good and uncommonly pretty, but as a young girl, I didn't understand her influence." Gisselle explained.

"Do you remember meeting any of her co-stars?" asked Kylan, gingerly pulling out scripts, one at a time. Leafing through them before carefully replacing them on the shelves.

"I met quite a few of them," she began. "Most of them have passed, but a few of her friends are still alive. I remember that she filmed a movie with Robert Wagner when I was quite young, and he used to come over quite a bit to rehearse with her, in private, away from the studio. They used to say they wanted to get their scenes just right because this movie had a touchy subject. In this interracial romance, the main characters' kids were adults. Even though they purported to be modern and inclusive, there was pushback. That's the role that she won the Oscar for."

"You know what," he said, "I know which movie you're talking about. They were seniors, who had fallen in love in college, but due to societal pressures, had married other people. Then, after each spouse had died, they found one another again, and she even had all his old love letters."

"That's the one," Gisselle smiled. "I wouldn't be surprised if she and Robert Wagner had some off-screen romance. He used to come over a lot."

"You don't say," Kylan chuckled. "Maybe we'll find some old love letters tucked between these scripts' pages."

"Wouldn't that be something," she agreed. When she had been fawning all over Kylan's home library the previous night, it hadn't occurred to her that her grandmother's study could constitute her own personal library, just housing works of a different kind. She wondered why she wasn't more impressed with herself. Watching Kylan actually take an interest in something that was part of the fabric of her life made Gisselle realize that perhaps she ought to give him a fair chance. After all, nobody was perfect, and he seemed sincere in his interest in her. Besides, he was an amazing kisser and seemed to have his life in good working order.

After several minutes, Kylan put the last script back on the shelf. "It would take me hours to look at everything here, Gisselle. It's getting pretty late, and I'm wondering if you'd agree to see me again, and maybe sometime you'll let me back in here to spend some more time looking at these amazing scripts."

"I'd like that very much," she said, "but I would also like the opportunity to revisit your library sometime."

"I look forward to that, I really do," said Kylan. He texted Atticus to come to pick him up from Gisselle's house. "It's getting late. My driver's on his way to take me home. I want to take you on a real date, where we schedule it, and I will pick you up and take you somewhere. Would that be okay?"

Gisselle laughed. "I would love that, Kylan. I think we're done with meeting up by accident. Here, let me give you my number."

He passed her his phone, and she keyed her name, number, and address into his contacts.

"What about tomorrow?" he asked. "It's Sunday. Do you have plans already, or are you free?"

"What did you have in mind?" she asked him with a gentle smile.

"" I'd like to take you out for an early dinner, maybe 6:00 p.m., then a trip to the observatory. Would you be interested in that?" He looked at her, trying to stay calm, waiting for her answer.

"That sounds amazing. Yes, I'd like that," Gisselle enthused.

"Perfect. Then I'll pick you up here tomorrow at 6:00 p.m." Kylan was trying really hard to keep from bubbling over with too much eagerness.

It was Gisselle's turn to come in closer to him, put her hands on his chest, and look up at his face expectantly. Kylan obliged by tipping his face down to kiss her. He loved how she tasted. He could already feel that their chemistry would be perfect. The feel of her lips was so soft and inviting, he knew he had a huge hard-on, and he didn't want Gisselle to feel it. Still, she pulled her body closer to his without concealing the obvious. She pretended not to notice, but she was secretly pleased with herself.

As their kiss deepened, Gisselle teased him slightly by thrusting her tongue deeper into his mouth and letting her hands caress his firm buttocks. Kylan was getting so turned on that he knew he needed to either tear off all her clothes and ravage her body right then and there, or he needed to get out.

"I have to go, Gisselle," his voice was almost panting.

She knew she was driving him wild and secretly loved it. However, she knew it would be even better if they got to know one another a little. Clearly, Kylan was already putting together a plan for tomorrow night. She didn't want to spoil it by being greedy tonight. After all, she thought, good things come to those who wait.

Gisselle pulled herself away from Kylan and led him back down the stairs. As she kissed him goodbye at the front door, she whispered into his ear, "Happy birthday, Kylan," and sucked his earlobe for a second.

It was hard for him to hold back, but maturity had taught him restraint. "Goodnight," he said, smiling, and got into his waiting limousine.

Gisselle closed the front door softly, then locked it shut. She realized she had been holding her breath. As she leaned her back up against the inside of the door, she let out a slow exhale, her eyes closed, trying to remember the feel of his lips against hers. She couldn't help it–she liked him.

She went upstairs to her room to undress, entered her en suite, and turned on her shower. Damn, Kylan was hot, she thought to herself. Part of her wished she could be as free-spirited now as her friend Indi. She had wanted to invite Kylan to spend the night and not in another bedroom. She would have done everything to that man and worked it, Missy Elliott style. Standing naked under her rainfall shower, she closed her eyes and remembered the heat she had felt when Kylan had been kissing her. He was definitely a good kisser, and she had a feeling he would be good at everything else, too.

Even if she was alone, she needed to have an orgasm tonight, or else she wouldn't be able to sleep–she'd fantasize about Kylan Murray all night long. Turning on the telephone shower attachment, she held it against herself in front of her vagina, letting the soft rhythm of the warm water pulse against just the right spot. With her free hand, she touched herself in the same rhythmic motion. Her eyes closed, and imagining that it was Kylan touching her. His fingers teasing her until she felt the waves of pleasure wash over her body, and it was over. Afterward, she dried herself off and got under the sheets, naked, imagining what it would feel like if Kylan were joining her in bed. She couldn't deny that the thought intrigued her.

Written in the Stars

GISSELLE AWOKE the following day feeling refreshed and optimistic. She realized that meeting Kylan Murray was a huge deal, and most women would be all over social media, bragging about it or obsessing over searching online for his personal information. She figured that Kylan was well-known enough, and had such a significant presence in the technology and venture capital sectors, that she didn't really feel the need to dig any further. His LinkedIn page looked legitimate, and his behavior and lifestyle seemed to back it up.

It was clear that the woman, Shay, in the Bar Marmont had some kind of a history with him, and she clearly wasn't ready to move on yet, but everyone has a past. She was in no position to judge because she had dated some serious jerks in the past, and sometimes it's hard to shake them loose. It's not easy to navigate the dating world, especially when you're known by reputation, as is the case with Kylan. Most women probably can't help but be star struck by his wealth and success. Then it prevents both parties from getting to know one another earnestly. Just like herself, when she met guys who already knew her family history, she had a hard time just relaxing because she always thought they were looking for industry connections through her parents. This is part of why establishing her reputation at The Elevated World was so meaningful to her.

Then again, embarking on a new relationship could be tricky. She shuddered as she remembered Leon. He was a police officer, and when they first met, he had been charismatic, gentle, and respectful toward her. However, after a few weeks of dating, Leon had become really possessive, making Gisselle quite uncomfortable. Then, one night a few months ago, Gisselle had caught a glimpse of his gray side. When he brought her home from a date, he had cornered her in her kitchen instead of being sweet. He had backed her up uncomfortably against the wooden cabinets using one arm to hold her. He accused her of cheating on him, called her an ugly whore, and poured a glass of water over her head.

Although Leon hadn't traditionally hit Gisselle, her body instantly knew that his intention had been to humiliate and abuse her, which is the cornerstone of an abusive relationship. At that moment, a flip switched inside of her. Filled with adrenaline, she had found tremendous strength to twist his arm away from her, break free, and run to the front door. Leon chased her and eventually followed her outside. She told him to go home, to never come back, and to lose her number. A voice inside her had told her that if she had let him hang around, the night could have ended very differently for her.

Usually, Gisselle didn't discuss her dating life with her parents unless the guy was really special. However, she immediately told them what had happened with Leon. Her mother immediately hired a private investigator to gather information about him and determine if they needed to be concerned. The PI provided a report indicating Leon was married, with two small children, and he lived in Encino with his wife, who worked as an accountant.

That's when Gisselle started filling in the blanks and realizing that Leon had been lying to her from the beginning. He had been as smooth and winsome as any man could be, and she liked that he was a detective. As a Black man working for the LAPD, she knew that he must have had to work diligently to be elevated to that position. However, the PI uncovered that his supposed residence in Westwood was actually an Airbnb he was renting. The revelation about him having a secret family suddenly made sense when she thought back and realized that there were certain times of the day when he didn't reply to her texts. It was because he was with his wife and children, not because he was out on a stakeout.

Although she could have gone to the police and had him charged with assault, Gisselle didn't want that on her conscience. If she filed a police complaint, that would mean the end of his career and, most likely, his marriage. Gisselle didn't want to be responsible for breaking up a family with two young children, however much Leon had wronged her. She found the strength within herself to forgive him. Still, she would never forget what he had done to her and never allow him, or anyone like him, into her life ever again.

Life was all about circles touching back, and Gisselle wanted to change the flow of energy and attract good karma. Besides, people like Leon eventually self-destruct all on their own. Gisselle wouldn't be around to see it happen, but ultimately, he would get his. She didn't need to be the one to stick it to him. She just hoped that the experience with her would have shaken him enough to realize that he can't treat women that way and expect to get away with it again.

That had been over six months ago, and she hadn't so much as flirted with anyone in the interim. Kylan was her first foray back into the dating game. She smiled a wry smile, imagining Indi would be so proud of her for landing a real date with Kylan. She thought he was spectacular. Gisselle only hoped that Indi's tryst with Pierce would last for a while because if not, things might get tricky between herself and Kylan. She had no doubt that as soon as Pierce went home, Indi would literally give her a blow-by-blow account of their wild and sexy night together. She laughed to herself and shook her head. At least one of them was having great sex.

Gisselle made a point to avoid looking at electronics until after her morning meditation session. She didn't check her phone before making herself a matcha latte, a slice of whole grain toast with almond butter, and a side of grapes. Looking out her kitchen window into her vast backyard, she couldn't help but think how lucky she was. The tennis court was inviting in the early morning light, and she wondered if Kylan played. She made a mental note to ask him because she knew he didn't have a tennis court on his property in Malibu. He might really enjoy hitting the clay with her. Maybe Pierce and Indi could come too, and they would play a doubles match. Or maybe she shouldn't get ahead of herself.

Looking over to the pool, her eyes fixed on the hot tub. She allowed herself to just rest on the mental image of Kylan, bare-chested, lifting his gorgeous, glistening body up out of the hot tub. She felt herself getting turned on; just thinking about the fun they could have in that pool together. When her grandmother was still alive, Gisselle would never have dared to go skinny dipping with a boyfriend in her pool. Now that she had the property all to herself, who could blame her. In fact, she was certain that in past decades, her grandmother had enjoyed her own very exciting swimming pool parties with any number of eligible gentleman friends.

Speaking of boyfriends, Gisselle's mind drifted back to thoughts of Kylan and at what point it was natural to start calling someone your boyfriend. They had only met two days ago, but as Gisselle had already spent the night at his home, one could argue that the path to relationship status had accelerated somewhat. Perhaps if she were to meditate on this question, her third eye would help her find clarity.

She picked up a rose quartz crystal from her bowl of magic rocks, as Indi called it, and headed into the solarium to sit on her yoga mat and find inner peace. The rose quartz was said to open your heart to receiving love, which is precisely what Gisselle wanted for herself at this moment in time. She sat down cross-legged on the mat, holding the crystal in her left hand, and began repeating her mantras:

Everything that I need, I already have
Everything that I have is all that I need
Anything I desire, I will receive
Because my reality is created by me
I am a powerful creator
I am pure positive energy
I radiate love
I am a masterpiece
I'm going to let myself enjoy my experiences
I am a confident queen
Positivity always wins

Gisselle could feel herself melt into her thoughts and sat peacefully in her meditative state. She felt strong, positive, and sure of herself. Her intuition told her that Kylan Murray was a very good man, and her gut was usually right. There were no niggling worries, no red flags, and no danger signs. He was just being very clear that he wanted to date her, spend time with her, and get to know her better. He wasn't playing games. He had admitted that he had seen her on The Elevated World's Twitter feed and that he found her very attractive. He had made an enormously generous donation to the organization. He wasn't shy to admit that he had insecurities. He was, in a word, normal, or at least as normal as a super-wealthy single man living in Los Angeles could be. As far as she could tell, he was "all in" where she was concerned. She felt it would be pretty difficult to fabricate all of that, and her glimpse into his character seemed legitimate.

After about ten minutes, she took herself out of her meditation and moved into a yoga flow. She had been practicing yoga for the past few years because even though it didn't provide the same kind of calorie burn as a run, yoga helped ease her stress. She also felt that it gave her good muscle strength and flexibility. She still enjoyed her cardio workouts, but yoga set the tone for her day. Today, she wanted to focus on the positive things that were happening in her life right at this moment. Her amazing job, her beautiful friends and family, and her potential new suitor. Those were big things to feel grateful for.

She wondered where Kylan was going to take her to dinner this evening. She was in the mood for sushi today, so if he asked her, she would tell him. Wouldn't it be great if they had the same tastes in food? Then what about after dinner? She wondered what he had planned for them. It sounded like he wanted to plan an official date night activity. He seemed like the well-organized type, which made sense because that would explain how he had become a self-made billionaire. He was clearly detail-oriented and likely very punctual.

Gisselle had a feeling that, if things went well on her date tonight, she might not make it into work the following day until the afternoon, so after lunch, she logged into the office server from home to complete some administrative tasks and prepare herself for what would likely be another busy week. As director of The Elevated World, she received notifications regarding all the donations over a certain threshold. In addition to Kylan's $500,000 donation from Friday night, she noted that he had pledged an additional $2,000,000 earlier that same day. Her mouth just gaped as she stared at the numbers on the screen. He was absolutely for real. The story he had told her, about having taken an interest in The

Elevated World, then seeing her picture on Twitter, he must be telling the truth. Gisselle sensed that Kylan was essentially just a bashful guy. He was highly successful in business, earnestly philanthropic, and just terrible at meeting women.

There was no word to use other than to say she felt relieved. Seeing that enormous donation validated her feelings of trust toward him. He was not some smarmy guy who picked up women in his limo and then wrote checks to impress them. Kylan was the real deal, and he was actually taking her on an actual date tonight. He was willing to date her, even after she pulled that rude disappearing act on Saturday morning. More and more, Gisselle felt that Kylan was worth her time and attention.

When she wrapped up her work, she moved on to considering her wardrobe. Tonight likely wasn't going to be formal, but it probably wasn't going to be overly casual, either. She would have to find an outfit that would strike a good balance between the two extremes, that would be suitable whether they went for tacos or lobster. She needed to be prepared to look good at museums or movies. Jeans were out of the question, even with a fancy top and great shoes, because it was just too warm outside. A slinky dress would make her look over-the-top at a 6:00 p.m. dinner. Then again, she didn't want to dress like she was going to a garden party, either.

After much consideration, Gisselle decided on a coral-colored, lace-trimmed satin wrap dress with cap sleeves and a mini-length hem. If she wore it with her gold wedge espadrilles, she would look dressed up but still daytime, which is the look she was going for. Kylan seemed to like her hair down, in all its natural afro glory, so she wasn't going to mess with that. As for her makeup, she chose a light layer of tinted pearlescent moisturizer to give her clear, youthful skin a glow. Then she added a wash of Nars Orgasm blush, some mascara, a sheer golden eye shadow, and a nude lip gloss. By the time

Kylan was due to pick her up, she was almost giddy with excitement.

Not wanting to appear obvious, Gisselle hid behind the drapes in the living room, stealthily looking out the window, watching for Kylan's limousine. However, instead of his usual chauffeured ride, Kylan pulled into her circular front driveway in a silver Mercedes convertible with a retractable hardtop. She let herself out the front door so that she could go meet him outside.

As Kylan stepped out of the vehicle, she took a good, long look at his handsome physique. He wore fitted chinos with a coral polo shirt, which was adorable because they practically matched. When they saw one another and noticed this, each of them smiled. His legs were long, and as he walked toward her to greet her with a kiss, Gisselle felt her heart give a little flutter. She was excited to see him, and his hello kiss didn't disappoint. If anything, it was a welcome preview of what she might experience later.

"So good to see you again," he said, looking straight into her eyes. "I've been thinking about you all day. Do you like sushi? I should have asked you. I made reservations at Nobu Malibu, but it's easy to change if you'd prefer something else."

"I love sushi," she told him as he held open the car door for her to get in. "I was just thinking. I hoped you felt like eating sushi tonight."

"Well then, I guess great minds think alike," Kylan replied as he got into the vehicle himself. "Are you okay with the top down?"

"Of course," she enthused, "there's nothing more fun on a hot day than a ride in a convertible."

As they drove out to Malibu, enjoying the glorious sunshine, Gisselle couldn't help but be turned on by the sight of Kylan's beautiful hands. His long fingers maneuver the six-speed stick shift. Most men couldn't drive sticks, but it was the mark of a dynamic man if he could drive a classic standard.

He noticed her looking at the gearshift and explained, "It's tough to find vehicles now with a standard transmission. I know it's more complicated, but I prefer the control that standard shift gives me, so I had to special order this car from Europe."

"That's cool," Gisselle answered. "I learned how to drive a stick shift when I was a teenager. My first car was a Mazda Miata."

"Nice," he appreciated her taste in sporty cars. "My other vehicles are all normal, automatic transmissions, a basic sedan and a sporty SUV, for when I want to take a trip down the coast or to the mountains."

"If they're your vehicles, then I doubt they're basic," she teased. "Is Sunday your driver's day off?"

"Yes, it is," Kylan replied, "but I prefer to drive ourselves today anyway. Having a driver is helpful during the workweek, when I have a long commute because I can work on my tablet in the back seat, or when I go out at night, and I want to imbibe a little."

"I get it. Better safe than sorry," she agreed.

The rest of the drive was easy, with a light conversation that tended toward the flirtatious. Gisselle was getting honest vibes off of Kylan. In her experience, the most successful guys were players. They tended to be serial monogamists, interested in you and making you feel special for a few weeks. Still, as soon as they noticed someone more interesting come along, the spell was broken, and they were suddenly gone. She wondered if Kylan was like that too, always searching for the next best thing. She supposed she would find out, but so far, he seemed natural and nice, talking about his parents, school experience, and philanthropy. He was also careful to ask her enough questions about herself so that he could learn a little bit about her background as well. He was conscious of her famous Hollywood roots and wanted to ask her enough questions to show his interest. But not so many as to appear as though he were prying. It was a delicate balance.

As they arrived at Nobu, Kylan parked the car himself, joking that the young valets didn't know how to drive a stick. They were seated at a beautiful, intimate table with a soothing ocean view. Kylan was aware that the other people in the restaurant, both men and women, were staring at Gisselle a little bit.

"You're too beautiful," Kylan told her. "All eyes are on you."

Gisselle laughed, 'You know what it is? It's because I look a lot like my mother and my grandmother. People stare at me sometimes because they're trying to place me and figure out where they know me from. Don't worry, it'll wear off."

"I hadn't thought of it from your perspective, but I think you must be right," he agreed. "You do look a lot like them. Enough to make people do a double take, I guess."

During their dinner, they talked about their goals, lives, and hopes for the future. They giggled a bit over Pierce and Indi getting together. Hoping that it would, at the very least, turn into a nice, fun friendship, even if it might not be their lifetime relationship. As long as they didn't wind up hating each other, which would make things awkward for future group socializing.

After Kylan paid the bill and they were getting up to leave, Gisselle started thanking him for dinner but was interrupted by Shay.

"Again, you're with her?" Shay demanded. "What's going on? Did you spend the whole weekend with this one? Is she your new flavor of the week? Is that it? Am I just trash to you now? Did you just dispose of me?" Her voice was just a notch too loud for the restaurant.

"Let's talk outside," Kylan kept his voice low and his tone cool.

"Shay, I'm sorry that you're unhappy with how things ended between us," he began, "But I just knew that we were headed nowhere. I'm truly sorry that you're so unhappy. Now, please let me enjoy my evening with Gisselle."

"But you won't even tell me why," she demanded.

Gisselle stood beside Kylan's vehicle, feeling awkward, just waiting for it to be over.

"Why? Will you really feel better when I tell you why? Will that give you closure? Because you're not getting another chance if that's what you're looking for," Kylan's tone was measured, but he could feel the fire rising up under his collar.

If Shay had been a cartoon, steam would have come out of her nostrils. Clearly, she didn't like the sound of his words, and she pivoted on one heel before stalking off in a huff.

When they got in the car, Gisselle cautiously asked him, "Do you want to tell me what happened between you two?"

Reluctantly, Kylan admitted that they had dated casually for a few months, going out about once a week. He hadn't trusted or liked her enough to bring her home, but he had taken her to hotels near his office. "Then, one night, I was out with Pierce, and I could tell he didn't really like her. He showed me her social media feed while we were having dinner. She had put me all over her Instagram, and she happened to be doing an Instagram Live story that was basically a how-to guide for landing a rich man."

"Oh dear, you don't say," Gisselle bit her lip.

"I had misgivings about her, which is why I had kept her at arm's length from the start," he went on. "It just goes to show you that when your gut tells you to keep away, and your best friend is saying beware, sometimes you should pause and reflect. I'm just glad I figured it out in time."

"Exactly," she agreed. "I'm sorry about our run-in with her. I hope it hasn't ruined our night."

"Not if I don't let it," he said with a wink, squeezing her knee. "Now, I had one other stop planned for us. Is that okay?"

"Sure, what did you have in mind?" she asked with a smile.

"I'm taking you to the Point Dume Observatory because books and stars are my jam," he explained. "Just so we're clear, you know you're out with a top-notch nerd, right?"

Gisselle giggled, "Got it."

As they pulled into the parking lot, the sky was getting dark enough to see the stars. Kylan walked her through the main building, explaining all the different stars and solar systems. There were also telescopes set up outdoors at the lookout point, and Gisselle couldn't help but notice a massive brick on the donor wall with Kylan's name carved into it.

"Let me show you the view through my favorite telescope," he suggested as he took her hand to guide her there.

Looking through the lens, Kylan pointed out Orion's Belt, the Big Dipper, and Draco. "When I was young, whenever I could get my hands on physics books or anything to do with astronomy or planetary movement, that's what made me tick."

"I did not know that you were into this sort of thing," Gisselle commented. "I like your hobbies."

"Look, whenever other boys used to make fun of me, I would resort to my physics books. I'd imagine myself building a rocket ship to take me away, all the way to the galaxy's outer edges. I would tell myself that one day, I would be able to buy and sell those bullies. Eventually, my intergalactic interest led me to develop apps that were picked up by NASA, so you might say that my love of books brought me here."

"Noted," she breathed as she turned to kiss him.

"Can I take you back to my place tonight?" Kylan paused

their kiss to ask her. "Or do you want me to drive you back home?"

"Your place," she whispered, and they left the observatory in a bit of a hurry.

It was a short drive along the beach to Kylan's house. They were kissing from the moment he pulled into the garage. The heat between them was palpable. Although they had only met a few days prior, a lot of pent-up sexual energy was simmering below the surface.

"Are you okay to spend the night in my room this time, in my bed?" he asked her gently.

"Yes, Kylan," she told him, without leaving any room for doubt. "Tonight, I'm all in."

As they made their way from the front entrance, through the living room, and down the stairs into Kylan's bedroom, they were leaving behind a trail of clothing, taking things off one at a time, trying not to break their kiss. Inevitably, their mouths parted long enough for Gisselle to help Kylan off with his polo shirt. Damn, his chest was fine, she thought to herself.

They were both already down to their underwear when they were inside his bedroom. As Kylan admired Gisselle's beautiful, lean, toned body in her delicate lace bra and panty set, he took a sharp inhale. Tonight was going to be amazing—for both of them. As they lowered themselves onto the bed, Kylan took a moment to open his nightstand drawer and retrieve a fresh box of condoms. Then he let his mouth travel down Gisselle's neck, kissing her gently down her arms to her wrists. He let his hands travel up her bare back to carefully unhook her bra, then took it off to reveal the most beautiful breasts he had ever seen. They were the perfect B cup size, and he softly stroked them with his hands, teasing her nipples before putting his mouth around them to start sucking. He took his time, licking and sucking her nipples before moving his mouth back to hers for another kiss while he moved his hands below.

Gisselle was wet before he had even started touching her. She was so incredibly turned on by his big, muscular body and take-charge attitude. She wanted him inside her at that moment, but she knew she should be happy that Kylan was into foreplay. Besides, there was nothing wrong with delayed gratification. As she let his fingers explore, her excitement was evident. She reached down to feel his big, hard shaft, which felt as smooth as velvet in her hands. He took a break from fingering her, and it was her turn to pleasure him.

Kneeling next to him on the bed, she bent her head down and took his penis in her mouth. Delicately, she let her tongue explore the head of his rock-hard penis, sucking and licking, while her hands moved gently up and down the shaft. Then with one hand, she cupped his balls and ever so gently tugged, then released. She then took his whole member in her mouth and moved her lips rhythmically up and down, up and down, pausing every once in a while to flick the tip and blow gently on it. She could tell he was close to coming when he asked her to stop.

He gently laid her on her back and kissed her nether regions to make sure that she was still turned on. He inserted two fingers into her vagina; wanting to be sure she would be ready to receive his mammoth cock. Then he kissed her down there, inflecting little licks and flicks. When he heard Gisselle say, "Please," he put on a condom, carefully positioned himself on top of her, and plunged so deep into her, as deep as he could possibly go. She moaned with pleasure. He thrust in and out, in and out, feeling her breath quicken to the point where he knew she was about to come. Kylan held back, allowing Gisselle to have her pleasure. Next, they turned over, with Gisselle straddling him. She moved back and forth and up and down, finally collapsing onto his chest as she felt her second orgasm ripple through her body. Finally, Kylan sat up, turned her around, and took her from behind. Now that she was totally relaxed, Gisselle just let herself lean into the gentle rhythm of Kylan's dick, moving slowly in and out of her, back and forth, slowly at first, and then more rapidly until he let go and had the biggest orgasm he could remember.

Their bodies rocked together for a few more moments, Gisselle appreciating the weight of his body on top of her, cradling her from behind before he finally pulled out and went into the en suite to dispose of the used condom.

"Gisselle, that was amazing," he said, returning to bed to kiss and cuddle her. "Would you consider spending the night with me?"

"Absolutely," she breathed, and they fell asleep in one another's arms, entirely spent.

The Morning After

NO REGRETS, thought Gisselle, as she woke up next to Kylan in his bed, relieved to know it wasn't a dream. He was already awake and tracing circles on her back with his hands. His touch was so electric that a simple movement could elicit this feverish warmth under her skin. She kissed him good morning and felt his mutual hunger for more.

"Before we get up, how about one more round?" he asked her.

She responded by kissing him more deeply and reaching down to feel the firmness of his cock. Obviously, he was ready, and Gisselle was very receptive to his sensual touch. Their love-making was slow and deliberate this morning, more patient than the night before. After petting her a little bit, Kylan put on a condom and slid easily inside. He stayed on top of her, missionary style, kissing her lips, neck, and shoulders as he thrust in and out. Their breathing started to synchronize, and when he could feel Gisselle clutching and panting, he knew she was close to the breaking point. He waited until he was sure, then he allowed himself to let go, and they came together.

Afterward, they lay together, kissing before each got out of bed to take a shower together.

As they were toweling off, Kylan offered to make her breakfast, which she accepted. They spent the time chit-chatting, and Kylan pointed out some early family photos. She liked this closeness that had developed between them and wondered when would be the right time to define their relationship status. Maybe she would first wait to see if he still wanted to keep seeing her before she got too far in her daydreaming.

"I see that we're both already late for the office," she noted, observing that it was already nine-thirty.

"I'm not worried about it," Kylan replied. "My first meeting isn't until the afternoon. I'm enjoying our time together now, but I respect your schedule if you have to leave."

"I do have to go, actually," said Gisselle ruefully. "I need to be there to attend to some things."

"In that case, may I ask Atticus to drive you home? Or straight to work? Just let him know what you prefer," Kylan offered.

"Thanks," she said. "I really appreciate that."

"Mmm, just give me one last kiss before you go, to give me a little something to keep me full until the last time I see you," he teased, and Gisselle obliged wholeheartedly.

Gisselle arrived home some time later, then changed and drove herself to work. She had been ignoring Indi's text messages all day for the simple reason that she didn't know what to tell her. Kylan hadn't mentioned anything about exclusivity, nor had he scheduled their next date. For all she knew, he might ghost her tomorrow. It wouldn't be the first time that she had misjudged someone. Finally, at the end of her workday, just as

Gisselle was pulling into her expansive circular driveway, Indi be-bopped across the front yard to greet her.

"Babe, where have you been?" Indi demanded, "I know you didn't come home last night."

"Oh, really?" answered Gisselle, "Were you checking up on me? I'm shocked you would have even noticed since I didn't think you and Pierce were ever coming up for air."

"Touché," said Indi wryly. "You have a point, and I must admit that meeting Pierce has been the perfect antidote to my cruel rejection by Nathan. We are seriously into each other; this isn't just a rebound fling. Pierce and I really get each other. He's smart and thinks I'm a breath of fresh air."

"I'm really happy for you, Indi," Gisselle told her friend. "Pierce does seem like a really good guy. A bit too much of a playboy for my taste, but very polite nonetheless."

"And hot, you can't ignore the fact that he's super fucking hot," Indi pointed out.

"Yes, he's absolutely on fire," Gisselle said with a laugh.

"But I'm very curious to know about your Kylan Murray," Indi wasn't giving up.

"Let me guess–you Googled him," Gisselle shook her head and wagged her finger at her friend.

"Of course I did," Indi freely admitted, "and I liked what I saw. Kylan checks out. He's an upstanding guy, he has an MBA, he's got credentials, and it even looks like he has no skeletons in his closet."

"Well, maybe just the one," Gisselle conceded. "Do you remember the woman who tried to crash our table at Bar Marmont? Shay Armstrong? Well, she tracked us down last night at Nobu Malibu. She confronted Kylan again."

"No, not possible," Indi was shocked and dismayed.

"Yes, very possible, actually," Gisselle went on. "Either Shay is seriously disturbed, or Kylan isn't telling me the truth about her."

"What do you mean by that?" Indi asked. "What did he offer you by way of explanation? Her behavior isn't normal or healthy by any means. So a man breaks up with you–that means it's over. You can't keep trying to make him date you. I take a different approach–when I'm done with them, I'm done with them, and when they're done with me, I'm over it. There's no need for further contact. It's not like they have kids."

"Right?" Gisselle agreed with her friend. "So Kylan told me they dated casually for a bit, and Pierce just couldn't stand her. Finally, Pierce showed Kylan how Shay had put images of him all over her Instagram feed, just full-on bragging." Indi's mouth was agape. "It gets better," Gisselle continued. "Then Pierce showed Kylan her Instagram live story, where Shay was giving women a lesson on how to land a rich man."

"Ew, that is so tacky," Indi said. "No wonder Kylan dumped her."

"Exactly," Gisselle paused before continuing. "The problem is that Kylan just seems too perfect, like tomorrow I'll wake up and realize that there's this other side to him that's going to disappoint me...."

"Disappoint you the way that Leon did," Indi finished her friend's sentence for her. "Look, Gisselle, Leon was an abusive guy, like off the charts with his psychological abuse and posses-siveness. I also believe that he suffered from a diagnosable personality disorder, which is reflected by the fact that you found out he was leading a whole double life."

"So you understand why I'd be reluctant to get involved with someone new." Gisselle was trying to articulate her misgivings, but there was nothing wrong with Kylan. He had been nothing but real, authentic, genuine, and honest with her. She liked that. Plus, he was great in bed.

"Look, Elle, you know I'll support you no matter what you do," Indi reassured her. "At some point, you'll be ready to discover that not every man out there will turn into another Leon. I actually think that Kylan is a legitimate catch, and he seems to adore you."

"Aaaargh... I know that you're right, Indi," Gisselle conceded. "Intellectually, I know that Kylan would make an amazing boyfriend. It's just that from an emotional standpoint, I feel that my life is so much simpler without romantic entanglements."

Indi looked at her, cocking her head to one side, and asked her friend, "How much fun did you and Kylan have last night, Elle? May I ask how many orgasms you've had within the past 24 hours?"

"Three," said Gisselle sheepishly, covering her eyes in mock shame.

"Girl," Indi laughed, "If that man gave you three solid orgasms last night, then I don't think any further discussion on this topic is required."

Pros

LATER THAT WEEK, after Pierce's clinic day ended, Kylan invited him to dinner at Mastro's Beverly Hills. They had texted each other a few times that week, just checking in as they always did. Pierce had been prodding him for information about his time with Gisselle. Still, Kylan had artfully dodged all his questions, preferring to have that conversation in person. Besides, Kylan felt that when it was someone he actually cared about, sending information tidbits to your friends by text was a bit juvenile.

"My brother," began Pierce, "You need to promise me that you won't screw anything up with your girl Gisselle because things are going so well between me and her little friend Indi. I don't want her to get upset if you drop Gisselle or something."

"Well, let's dive right into this conversation, then, and skip the small talk," Kylan chuckled. "You have nothing to worry about, Pierce, I promise. I have to tell you that it has been very long since I was this deep into a woman. It's like she's magic because the more time I spend with her, the more I crave. Like, I just can't get enough of her. Do you know what I mean?"

"Wow, Kylan, the sex must be outstanding, hey?" Pierce

couldn't help himself from asking. Then, seeing the look on Kylan's face, a look that said, I might marry this woman, so we're not going to talk about what she's like in bed, Pierce changed the tone of the discussion. "Wait a minute–am I hearing what I think I'm hearing? Are you starting to fall in love with Gisselle? Miss Old Hollywood?"

"I've only known her a week, but I think I'm in love with her," Kylan replied thoughtfully. "You know, everything is just easy and fun with her. We can talk about anything. She's happy, selfless, driven, and just an impressive human being." He lost himself in his thoughts, picturing her bright eyes and gorgeous smile. "I really care about her, man. In fact, I've invited her to spend the weekend with me in Catalina."

"Oooh, a whole weekend together, no breaks. I can see that the train has left the station. Well, I certainly got a good feeling from her," said Pierce. "She's not an insane gold digger like Shay, that's for sure, and I'd call that a plus."

"You're right about that," Kylan agreed. "I don't know how Shay manages to find me everywhere I go. I feel like she may have installed a GPS tracker on my phone, or maybe she's hired someone to follow me, or there's a mole in my office telling her what's in my calendar because she just shows up everywhere. On Sunday night, for example, she practically accosted me at Nobu. It made Gisselle really uncomfortable."

"Shay's behavior is just bizarre. She has zero self-respect. Women used to throw themselves at me when I was in med school. Still, nothing ever came close to what you're getting from Shay," Pierce was as puzzled by her behavior as Kylan was. "Oh, shit," he said, "Incoming."

Kylan turned around to see Shay Armstrong sashaying up to their table. She wore leather leggings, a halter top, and super high platform heels. Her breasts were practically bursting forth from her top. She just oozed sex in a way that Kylan found utterly unappetizing. He shook his head a little, suppressing an "ugh" sound, and shuddering at the thought that he had ever found Shay attractive. Everything about her was totally déclassé. Shay was the antithesis of Gisselle. Thank God he had dodged that bullet–or had he?

Shay stood between the two men, apparently waiting for an invitation to sit down with them. Unfortunately for her, no such invitation was forthcoming. Kylan and Pierce were becoming increasingly uncomfortable with Shay's presence. Kylan was starting to wonder, for real, if Shay was tracking him, the thought of which quite unnerved him.

"Excuse me, please," said Pierce, excusing himself from the table. "I'm going to the men's room so the two of you can speak privately. When I return in two minutes, Shay, I will resume my seat at the table, and you'll be gone."

Kylan admired his friend's direct approach. When Pierce walked away, Shay didn't waste time lighting into Kylan. "I'm still waiting for an explanation, Kylan. You just left me high and dry. I expected more from you."

"Look, Shay, I've said this before, and I'll repeat it," Kylan was struggling to remain cool and detached and not show her how annoyed he was by her behavior. "You and I had some fun together, and when we dated, all I was really down for was a good time. I stopped seeing you because I realized I just don't trust you. We don't have a real emotional connection between us. I'm sorry that you're disappointed, but if I'm going to spend time with someone, she needs to be a woman of substance, someone with whom I connect on a spiritual level. That person isn't you."

As Kylan spoke to her, he saw that Shay was visibly upset. Clearly, she had a lot of pride invested in dating Kylan, and she felt like she's received some kind of injury to her ego. Kylan knew there couldn't be any real feelings because he had watched her Instagram Live with his own eyes. The way she had spoken about him, it was like he wasn't even a human being, just an asset or a toy. Now, Shay would have to find another mark to scam.

As Pierce returned from the restroom, Shay got out of the chair, clearly holding back her rage. Kylan felt that if she were Medusa, he would have been turned to stone from the look of plain hatred in her eyes.

"You'll regret doing this to me," promised Shay. "You just be careful now, and remember that Hell hath no fury...."

"Like a woman scorned," Pierce finished the sentence as Shay walked away. "Jesus, Kylan, of all the bitches in L.A., you had to get mixed up with that one?"

"Tell me about it," Kylan said ruefully. "Now that she's gone, we can relax and enjoy a nice, normal dinner. I think our food is about to arrive."

"Until then, we need another round of drinks," said Pierce, motioning to their server. "Two scotch, neat, please."

Flipping the Script

ON THURSDAY, to say that Gisselle had been floating on air all week would be an understatement. She hadn't seen Kylan since Monday morning, but he had called and texted her several times a day. Plus, he had invited her away with him for this coming weekend. He would pick her up on Friday afternoon, and they would sail to Catalina. Kylan had chartered a motor yacht with a small crew, and the plan was to sail there, moor, and then go for romantic day trips to the island. Just the two of them would be so amorous for the whole weekend together. She laughed when he assured her, remembering having seen Natalie Wood's autograph on Gisselle's fireplace mantle, that their boat wouldn't be called The Splendor and promised to bring her home safely. She couldn't wait to tell Indi all about their weekend getaway plans.

Her relationship with Kylan moved forward in a way she hadn't experienced before. Maybe it was their natural chemistry or mutual interests that enabled their conversations to flow freely and easily. There was no holding back, and each wanted to learn as much as possible about the other. They had talked on the phone for about an hour every night, old-school, on their landlines, and wishing one another goodnight before putting their heads down on their pillows. This type of relationship throwback activity took her back to a simpler, happier time in her life. All she wanted was to hold on to that feeling of physical and emotional safety that she felt with Kylan.

Gisselle believed there was a real connection, a tangible bond, forming between the two of them. She felt that this would turn into the relationship of a lifetime, and she didn't know how to explain it. Maybe it was because, at age 31, Kylan was looking around at the state of his life. Enjoying his career success and realizing that he wanted to share it with someone in a significant, perhaps more permanent, way. As for her, she wasn't actively seeking a life partner, but some of her friends were starting to get married, and she pictured her future life with Kylan. It could happen, she thought to herself. Maybe she would meditate on that future happy thought and manifest it, and then it would come true for her.

It seemed to Gisselle that everything was going so well for her suddenly. She was still kind of in shock over Kylan's major gifts to The Elevated World. The board members to whom Gisselle was responsible as the director had all sent her emails congratulating her outstanding fundraising efforts, which had put the charity further ahead than it had ever been in the fiscal year. She knew that financial stability was key for the organization to continue providing literacy support and hiring the right people. Kylan's generosity would play a major role in the succession plan of the charity.

Now that the workday was almost over, Gisselle would finally have the opportunity to tell Indi about her weekend plans with Kylan. She decided to call her and see if her friend was free to join her at the gym after work. "Indi," she said, "Are you free to meet me at Equinox in an hour?"

"I'm just wrapping up, so it's perfect timing," replied Indi.

"Great," Gisselle knew she needed to plan her weekend outfit choices with Indi in person. "See you there."

Thank goodness she had been able to squeeze in a full leg and bikini wax over her lunch hour. She knew that she would spend a lot of time this weekend in her bathing suit, in the sunlight, on the boat, and she wanted her skin to be as smooth and inviting as possible. It sounded juvenile, but she wanted to be as perfect as she could be for Kylan. A weekend away with her new man was exciting, and she wasn't going to deny herself that childlike enthusiasm. She let herself believe that someday, they would refer back to this weekend as their very first getaway together.

At Equinox, Gisselle got onto an elliptical in her usual workout spot. While working out, she opened a fashion magazine to read on the built-in rack. After about fifteen minutes, Indi hopped onto the machine next to her. She was ready to hear all the exciting details about Kylan.

"Indi, he's taking me to Catalina this weekend. He rented a yacht," Gisselle began.

"No way!" Indi couldn't contain her excitement. "That is so sexy. You're going to have such an amazing time. Does this mean you're official?"

"I don't exactly know," Gisselle admitted. "We talk and text all the time, and I'm pretty sure he's not seeing anyone else, but I haven't come out and asked him to define our relationship."

"Well, it shouldn't be that difficult," Indi said. "He's in his thirties. He's an accomplished businessman. He should be secure enough in his position to be able to call you his girlfriend."

"I'm actually not that concerned about it," Gisselle replied. "I'm pretty sure that we're a couple. He's been very open and honest with me. After what happened with that woman, Shay, I definitely don't think he would lead me on. I think that whisking me away for an entire weekend, just the two of us is a sign of commitment in itself."

"I agree with you," said Indi. "You had better have a ton of fun and don't you dare disappoint me. Any chance he's mentioned that his good friend Pierce can't get enough of me?"

Gisselle laughed. "Well, actually, he did tell me that Pierce usually likes to 'hit it and quit it as they say, but he seems to really like you a lot. According to Kylan, Pierce has full-on mentionitis. He just can't stop talking about you, and that's a good thing."

"Hmm, then I wonder when Pierce will be planning a weekend getaway for the two of us?" Indi pondered.

"My guess would probably be when he's not on call at Cedars-Sinai Medical Center," laughed Gisselle.

After their workout, they both showered and got dressed again before leaving. They planned to return to Gisselle's house together, order delivery, and go through Gisselle's wardrobe choices for her romantic weekend away, including some memorable lingerie selections. As they were heading out the front doors, Shay rushed up and stopped Gisselle, practically getting in her face. Immediately, Gisselle felt the bile rise in her throat. Shay's accosting her like this was way offside and more than a little distasteful.

"There's something you need to hear–" Shay had stepped right in front of Gisselle, just beside the front doors.

Indi just stood there, her mouth agape. Gisselle was really uncomfortable. It felt like she was being stalked.

"Look, Shay," she began, "I've tried to be patient and sensitive, but you're really taking things too far by following me around. I'm sorry that things didn't turn out as you had hoped, but you need to leave me out." Gisselle's tone was polite but firm.

"But you don't understand," said Shay defensively. Then,

she held up her phone and played a recording of Kylan saying, "all I was really down for was a good time."

Gisselle heard what he said, but she didn't show it if she was bothered by those words. "And? Shay, as far as I understand, Kylan and I met after you two had broken up. I've done nothing wrong, and neither has Kylan."

"Wanna bet?" Shay just wasn't going to give up. "Girl, I've been looking for you all over town because I need to warn you about the plague that is Mr. Kylan Murray. He will wine you, he will dine you, he will take you on a plane, and he will take you on a yacht. He will toss you out like yesterday's trash when you get comfortable and move on to the next."

"And you're telling her this because?" Indi interjected.

"Because she needs to keep herself safe from this plague of locusts that is Kylan Murray. Trust me when I say that man is a serial dater, and he'll never put a ring on it. Honey, you'll be lucky if he even remembers your name after next week," Shay said bitterly before proceeding to open up her phone to show Gisselle a series of about twenty photos, all appearing to be recent, of Kylan smiling with his arm around a different woman each time.

Gisselle looked at the images briefly, but Indi took a closer look. Something about this whole situation didn't sit right with her. "Alright, Shay," she said. "You've said your piece, and you've done your damage. Now please leave us alone."

With that, Shay finally walked away, throwing up her hands as if to say, I tried.

Indi and Gisselle got into their vehicles and headed to Gisselle's house. Once they got there, Indi could tell that Gisselle had been adversely affected by what Shay had said to her. However, Indi wasn't convinced that Shay's claims were credible. There was something about those images she had shown, Kylan posing with all those women. They were all practically the same pose, in the same lighting. It just didn't make sense, not based on what she had gathered about Kylan so far, and totally inconsistent with how he treated Gisselle. She knew that if she kept thinking about it, she would figure it out eventually.

"Elle," she offered softly, "Do you still want to put together your weekend capsule wardrobe?"

"You know what, Indi," Gisselle replied, somewhat resignedly, "I think tonight I'm good." Indi hugged her friend goodnight and made her way silently home.

The Fury

LATER THAT SAME NIGHT, Kylan phoned Gisselle, as per usual, to have their goodnight talk. He had some ideas for their trip to Catalina, and he was excited to talk to her about them and find out what activities she wanted to do and if there were any special restaurants she wanted to try. However, Gisselle didn't answer her landline when he called. He also tried texting her. When it got close to 10:00 p.m., he worried that she wasn't responding to his texts, nor was she answering her home phone or her cell.

He called Pierce to see if he had heard anything from Indi about her and Gisselle going out together. It was strange, though, because Gisselle had simply mentioned that she was going to the gym after work and then coming home.

"Man, I just got off the phone with Indi," Pierce began. "I'm just going to start by saying that Indi is on your side, man, but that Shay bitch, she's out of control."

"Shit, Pierce, what happened now? Please don't tell me that Shay went and did something to Gisselle today at work," now Kylan was starting to become concerned.

"Worse, my brother," Pierce went on. "Shay went to find

Gisselle and practically pounced on her as she left Equinox. Man, on the street, in front of passers-by, and Indi was just standing there, not knowing what to do. Shay started showing Gisselle like a hundred pictures of you with your arms around all these different women."

"What the hell?" Kylan was in total disbelief.

"Don't you remember, at Mastro's, she warned you that she was going to get even with you," Pierce reminded him. "She even said that Hell hath no fury like a woman scorned."

"Oh, God, how can I forget?" Kylan was beside himself. "That woman is a lunatic."

"She told Gisselle that you're a player, a serial dater and that you were going to ghost her next week and move on to bigger and better things," Pierce said. "Indi told me that Gisselle was freaked out. She had a bad relationship where the guy wasn't who he said he was, and he had a whole secret family, something crazy like that."

"And now she thinks I have a secret life that she doesn't know anything about, am I right?" asked Kylan, completely deflated.

"That's pretty much it. Indi told her not to listen to Shay, but I don't know, man," continued Pierce. "You might want to go see her. Maybe get a restraining order against Shay because her actions will result in total social impairment for you. Jeez."

"Right, man, thanks. I'll let you know what happens," Kylan said as he hung up the phone.

Kylan was completely dumbfounded. He had no clue what he had done wrong. As far as he could tell, things had been progressing really well with Gisselle. She appreciated his sense of humor, he liked her quirks, and he was even starting to buy into her philosophy about crystal energy. From his standpoint, it was all systems go, and now Gisselle was buying what Shay was selling and had stopped answering his calls. All this happened just when he was on the verge of asking her to get serious with him. He had planned on discussing mutual exclusivity while they were enjoying some romantic time on the yacht. Now, instead of looking forward to their first weekend alone together, Kylan felt like his one chance at real happiness was about to slip away.

Without wasting any more time, Kylan got into his car and drove for almost an hour to finally arrive outside Gisselle's home in Hancock Park. He could see that there were still lights on inside, which meant that she hadn't yet gone to sleep. He rang the bell and knocked on the door, calmly persisting until she finally opened the door. He noticed her eyes looked puffy and red, as if she had been crying.

"I thought you were different," she said, her voice catching a little. "I just can't do this tonight, Kylan. I'm sorry."

She closed the door again before Kylan could respond. All he could do was walk back down the long driveway, get into his vehicle, and drive away.

As soon as Kylan woke up the following day, he asked Atticus to drive him to Shay's office. She worked in a large accounting firm in a building in downtown Los Angeles that wasn't far from his own office. When he arrived at the reception, he didn't even need to introduce himself because the receptionist knew exactly who he was. She phoned Shay to come out front immediately.

Shay walked out into her firm's waiting room, gloating at the sight of Kylan there waiting for her. "Well, to what do I owe this lovely visit, Kylan, darling? It's really been too long, hasn't it?" she cooed in a devilish voice.

"I know what you've done, and I don't understand why

you thought it was a good idea," Kylan said, struggling to maintain his composure.

"Why sir, I don't know what you're talking about," Shay said, batting her eyelashes at him in an unsuccessful attempt to emulate Mae West. "All I did, sugar, was I warned her what her fate would be if she continued down this path of a mock relationship with you. Let me tell you, she did not like the picture I painted, no sir."

Kylan thought about what he would say in response to Shay's inane words but instead remained silent, turned on his heel, and left without speaking to her again. He would be able to salvage his relationship with Gisselle. He just had to have faith that sincerity would win out in the end.

Here Comes the Rain

As soon as Kylan left Shay's office building, he asked Atticus to drive him to The Elevated World. He wasn't quite sure yet what his plan would be, but he was desperate to make things right with Gisselle, who still hadn't replied to any of his text messages from that morning. When he arrived, the front desk advised him that Gisselle was working remotely that day and wouldn't be coming in.

He returned to his limousine and asked Atticus to drive him to Gisselle's house. He knew that he wasn't giving up. He needed Gisselle to see the truth about him, which was nothing like the picture that Shay had painted of him. During the drive, he emailed his assistant, asking her to cancel his meetings for the day as he had an important personal matter to attend to.

It was one of those late spring days in Los Angeles. The forecast called for high temperatures and sunshine, with intermittent showers. Just as they arrived at Gisselle's home, the rains began. Kylan hadn't brought a raincoat, so he held his suit jacket over his head to keep himself dry. Gisselle heard the limo drive up, and she got up from where she was sitting in the living room, then started to close the drapes.

Their eyes met, and Gisselle couldn't help it. Her face softened immediately, and she felt a rush of emotions. She didn't want to break up with him. Every bone in her body was telling her to ignore what Shay had said about him, and to rely on her gut instinct, which was telling her that Kylan was as honest as they come. She stood inside the window, watching Kylan, waiting for her to give him a sign. He was getting thoroughly drenched. After what seemed like an eternity, she gestured for him to go to the front door.

By the time Kylan had walked to the front door, he was entirely drenched from his head down to his shoes. Gisselle didn't care because she knew that only a man with a pure heart would keep trying this hard to be a part of her life.

"Please, let me explain something to you," he began. "There is no other woman like you. Years ago, when I was a senior in college, I thought that I had found the love of my life. We shared our hopes and dreams, and I told her about the first app I planned to develop. Instead of staying with me, she went and got together with one of my professors, who stole my app idea and my woman."

"Why are you telling me all this?" Gisselle asked him. "What does any of this have to do with me?"

"I'm trying to tell you that I know what it feels like to be betrayed by someone you trust. I know what that feels like, and I would never want you to feel that way. I don't want to ever hurt you, Gisselle," he vowed. "I mean that."

Just then, Indi burst through the front door, which Gisselle had neglected to lock. "Elle, I figured it out!" she bellowed as she stormed in. She stopped when she saw that Kylan was there.

"Am I interrupting something?" she asked ruefully.

"It's fine," said Gisselle. "What did you figure out?"

"The pictures that Shay showed us, with all the women," Indi said excitedly. "I figured it out because I do hair and makeup and know wardrobe. Kylan was in the same hair and makeup, the same clothes, and even in the same lighting for every one of those snapshots. That's what was bugging me this whole time. I think Shay used Photoshop to doctor all those images. There's no way you'd wear a salmon pink vee neck sweater for a date with twenty different women, am I right?"

Kylan smacked his forehead. "No," he began, "It wasn't Photoshop. I know exactly what you're talking about. I gave a lecture to a female entrepreneurial networking group a couple of months ago, and I was wearing a salmon cashmere sweater. Everyone wanted to pose for a picture with me after my talk."

"You're kidding me," said Gisselle. "So you mean to say that I fell for Shay's desperate trick and missed out on a whole extra day of being your lover?"

"So it would seem," said Indi. "Now, Kylan, you must go home and clean yourself up because I believe you're taking my best friend to Catalina this afternoon."

Gisselle gave him a kiss so deep that he would forget the past 24 hours. Kylan left and made plans to pick her up in a few hours.

"Girl," said Indi, "I think we need to go upstairs and get you packed."

Come as You Are

"I COULD GET USED TO THIS," Gisselle said, nuzzling Kylan's neck as they cuddled on the yacht's top deck, enjoying a glass of prosecco and feeding one another grapes. As soon as they had reconciled, the rain stopped. It was almost poetic. The sun had started shining again, warming their skin, and the ocean air was fresh and warm.

"You can feel free to get used to this, my darling because if you want to be a yacht girl, I can make you my yacht girl," Kylan laughed.

"I really just want to be your girl," she said. "I like the yacht part, but just spending time with you is good enough for me."

"Thank you for believing in me. I promise never to let you down," he said softly, kissing her. "All I wanted to do, from the moment I first laid eyes on you, was to take care of you, make you my woman. I want you with me all the time, every day, with no breaks in between."

"That can be arranged," she replied, kissing him back.

Both of them had experienced the full range of emotions that day. Each of them feared that their relationship was over, however beautiful it could have been. Now, they were full of hope for their future because they knew that if they could wholeheartedly trust one another, they would ultimately endure as a couple. It was what both of them wanted, more than anything. When Kylan wrapped his arms around her, Gisselle felt treasured when she knew that there was no faking that kind of affection.

Truth be told, Gisselle had been embarrassed by her behavior over the past day. She shouldn't have let Shay get under her skin and trusted Kylan's sincerity. It wasn't like her to be swayed by unsubstantiated evidence, but at least they had managed to get to the truth of the matter.

Without realizing it, Gisselle had unfairly projected all her relationship fears onto Kylan, and there was no reason for it. While she had been badly hurt in the past, she needed to recognize that the abuse she experienced with Leon was a learning experience. She had gained much wisdom since that time. She was better equipped now to identify red relationship flags. Instead of finding fault with Kylan, she should have questioned Shay's sincerity. Kylan had been consistent and kind from the moment they met. He had never given her any reason to doubt him. She knew better now. Kylan was her Prince Charming come to life. She marveled at how lucky she was to live a real-life fairy tale.

After just a week together, they knew that their relationship was moving quickly. However, they were both at a point in their lives where they knew themselves well enough to understand what was important for the longer term. They had already decided that they would meet one another's parents the following weekend and, hopefully, bring both families together after that. Kylan had half-jokingly expressed some concern that his parents would be star-struck. Nevertheless, this natural progression felt very right to them.

"Who would have thought that Pierce and Indi would

have been the glue that would hold us together?" Kylan mused.

"That's right–they never gave up on us. They were determined to see us through," Gisselle smiled as she remembered the look of utter joy on her friend's face when she had figured out the issue with the photographs. "She wasn't buying Shay's story from the start."

"You know what?" he said, "I think we should agree to not mention her name again, okay? Let's just forget that unpleasantness ever happened, and put our faith where it belongs. In each other. What do you say?"

"I say, 'Aye, aye, Captain,'" laughed Gisselle, leaning in for another kiss as they sailed into the sunset, on their maiden love voyage.

In *Unmasking the Billionaire*, a dating site matches Javon and Lydia. They fall hard and fast. The problem is... Javon never told her that he's a billionaire.

Start reading now!

Other Books by Rose M. Cooper

About the Author

Rose M. Cooper read her first novel when she was eight years old. Since then, she has read tens of novels and twice as many short stories. She, however, did not discover her special knack for writing romance fiction until a decade later.

Now a full-time author with a specialty in contemporary romance, Cooper writes sensual yet relatable love stories designed to hook her readers at first glance. She views writing as another outlet to creativity, and thus has no intentions of setting down her pen just yet. There are many intriguing love stories to be told, and Cooper is set to tell them all.

She hails from New York and currently makes her home in Copiague, New York with her husband, her black cat and her Maine Coon cat. When she is not writing, you will most certainly find her around computers or getting her nose stuck in a book.

facebook.com/RoseMaeCooper

twitter.com/rosemaecooper

instagram.com/rosemaecooper

tiktok.com/@rosemaecooper

amazon.com/author/rosemaecooper

Sign Up For My Newsletter To Receive New Release Updates & Specials!

rosemaecooper.com/newsletter

THANKS FOR READING THIS BOOK. PLEASE CONSIDER LEAVING A REVIEW WITH YOUR RETAILER!

www.ingramcontent.com/pod-product-compliance
Lightning Source LLC
Chambersburg PA
CBHW022035170626
46808CB00003B/1217